Cupid:
The Bewildering Bequest

J. M. Jeffries

CUPID: THE BEWILDERING BEQUEST
Published by ImaJinn Books, a division of ImaJinn

First Printing March, 2000

ISBN: 1-893896-06-4

Cover design by Patricia Lazarus

ImaJinn Books, a division of ImaJinn
P.O. Box 162, Hickory Corners, MI 49060-0162
Toll Free: 1-877-625-3592
http://www.imajinnbooks.com

Dedication:

Jackie Hamilton: Many thanks to Miriam. So what if we didn't get it right the first time. Jennifer Baby, thanks for slapping the 'baby.' Linda, you are a Goddess with a big 'G'.

Miriam Pace: Dedicated to the loyal members of the Inland Valley Chapter RWA. Without their terrific support and clear vision, Jackie and I might never have come as far as we have.

To Roberta, thank you for feeding us when we didn't want to take a break.

To my Dad for driving 1500 miles to help around the house and do all the little things that never seem to get done so that I had the freedom to work.

TO OUR READERS

Join the Cupid Club.
Contact J.M. Jeffries at: CupidClub@yahoo.com
and receive a bi-annual newsletter and a free gift.

Note from ImaJinn Books

Dear Readers,

Thank you for buying this book. The authors have worked hard to bring you a captivating tale of love and adventure.

In the months ahead, watch for our fast-paced, action-packed stories involving ghosts, psychics and psychic phenomena, witches, vampires, werewolves, angels, reincarnation, futuristic in space or on other planets, futuristic on earth, time travel to the past, time travel to the present, and any other story line that will fall into the "New Age" category.

The best way for us to give you the types of books you want to read is to hear from you. Let us know your favorite types of "other world" romance. You may write to us or any of our authors at: ImaJinn Books, P.O. Box 162, Hickory Corners, MI 49060-0162. You may also e-mail us at imajinn@worldnet.att.net.

Be sure to visit our web site at: http://www.imajinnbooks.com

Prologue

Rain cascaded down the windshield, so heavy the wipers could barely handle it. Jason Stavros leaned forward, wiping a porthole in the steam on the inside of the glass. He tried to peer through the blinding deluge. If the rain didn't stop soon, he'd be late for Miss Eulalie Bidwell's funeral. This was his last chance to pay the proper respect for the woman who had saved his life.

A gust of wind caught his truck and slid it to the right of the slippery road. His wheels scraped the curb. He corrected the truck and continued on, no faster than a baby's crawl. Hurricane Abigail had hit the South Carolina coast with a vengeance that morning, and the old girl refused to go quietly, bringing the entire city of Charleston practically to a halt.

Water sprayed to either side of the truck. Through the blast, Jason saw another car parked on the side of the road, trapped in a huge puddle. The car listed to one side and he could see a frail old man trying to lift the spare tire out of the trunk. The old man was drenched, his wispy, white hair plastered to his skull. Jason parked behind the old car, knowing he needed to help.

He pulled his umbrella from the back seat. The umbrella had been a gift from Miss Eulalie, who'd worried his native New York blood wasn't strong enough to withstand the downpours Charleston regularly received, nor the humidity which left him soaked and drained of energy.

He opened the door, clicked open the umbrella and held it over himself as he slipped out of his jacket, threw it back into the car, and trudged through the rising water toward the old man. Rain filled his shoes, soaking his socks.

When Jason reached him, the old man shrugged and said, "Flat tire."

He continued to struggle with the spare. His clothing was as old and decrepit as his car. Jason hadn't known anyone still owned an Edsel. The rust bucket looked held together with baling wire, electrical tape, and a lot of good intentions.

"Let me take care of this." Jason handed the umbrella to the old man. "Why don't you wait inside the car out of the rain?"

The old man took the umbrella. "You're all dressed in your Sunday best, young man. I can manage this tire. I'm stronger than I appear. No need for you to get yourself dirty on our account."

Deciding the old guy was about five minutes away from falling over with a heart attack, Jason gently eased the man toward the curb. "I insist."

The passenger door flew open, and a fragile looking, elderly woman stepped out. Gray hair, pulled severely back into a tight bun, framed a worn, lined face. Her brown oxford shoes slid into a puddle, and her faded flower print dress wrapped around her legs like a wet sheet. "Cornelius Cupidano, what is taking so long about that tire?"

Mr. Cupidano waved his hand. "Vena, you hush up. This nice young man is going to help us."

Vena glanced up at the sky. Suddenly, the rain stopped, and a ray of sunshine parted the thick clouds. She smiled at Jason, her blue eyes bright and sparkling. Her face seemed to shimmer, and for a second, he'd swear she grew younger and more sensual. She threw Jason a look so hot, he thought his briefs would catch fire.

He blushed, embarrassed by the old girl trying to vamp him. What was she thinking about? She was old enough to be his grandmother's grandmother!

"Hello, young man." Her voice was a sensual purr. She tossed him a finger wave. He noticed rings decorating each one of her fingers.

"Hi." Jason rolled up his shirt sleeves, preparing to do battle with the tire.

Vena sashayed up to him and ran her finger down the front of his shirt. "Aren't you a pretty one?"

"Uh...thank you." She flirted so outrageously, Jason did a double take. This woman must have been hot in her day. The old man had been lucky to get her. He bet their marriage was still filled with fire. Jason had thought he'd had the same passion in his marriage. Boy, had he been wrong.

The old man stomped over, grabbed the lady's arm and pulled her away. "Vena, you let this boy be. He's doing us a good turn."

Vena pouted at Jason, her eyes twinkling. "He never lets me have any fun." She blew Jason a kiss, her bright red lips quivering with laughter.

Jason was so floored, his mouth gaped open. Then he remembered his offer of help. He pulled out the jack. Ten minutes later, he tightened the lug nuts and put the flat in the trunk.

"You really need to buy some new tires. These are just about bald." He slammed the trunk closed. "Tucker's Automotive on Ocean Avenue is having a big sale this weekend. My name is Jason Stavros. Tell Nate Tucker I sent you. He'll give you a good deal."

"You're so sweet, Jason Stavros. Thank you." Vena tilted her head flirtatiously and winked.

Her husband nudged her. "Stop that, you old tart. You're embarrassing the boy."

"Thank you, dear." She kissed her husband's cheek with a loud smack. "I do my best."

"Now get in the car." The old man pointed. "We have work to do."

"Well." Before getting into the car, she turned and gave Jason another little finger flutter. "Bye." She blew him a kiss.

Jason had the sensation of something light and sweet landing delicately on his cheek. The sweetness seemed to spread and grow, filling him with such happiness he suddenly wanted to dance.

"See you around," he told the woman.

"Thank you, young man." Cornelius Cupidano walked over to him. "How much do I owe you?"

"Nothing, sir. It was my pleasure to help you."

The old man waved his hand in the air. "No, I have to pay. I insist." He reached into his pocket and pulled out a little leather pouch.

On the side, a bow and arrow inside a heart was embossed in gold. What an odd little pouch. Jason heard the clinking of coins hitting each other as the old man peered inside. He jingled the bag.

Jason couldn't take his eyes away. He could swear little sparks shot out of the bag. He shook his head, deciding he was just imagining things.

The old man put his fingers inside the bag, slowly withdrew a gold coin and held it out to Jason. "Take it."

Jason hesitated. After having Serena for a wife, he knew what real gold looked like. He glanced at the car. The muffler hung from coat hangers, and the driver's door didn't quite close all the way. "Sir, I can't take your money." If he took the coin, these people might not eat for a lot of tomorrows.

"Nonsense." The old man grabbed Jason's hand and deposited the coin in his palm. "You take this coin. I have more." He closed Jason's fingers around the coin, and Jason felt a jolt go up his arm and down his spine, leaving him feeling as if he'd been punched.

For a second, he couldn't think, couldn't breathe. The old man shuffled to the driver's door and turned around. "You keep that coin, young man. You keep it with you all the time, and you'll always have good luck."

The old man climbed inside the car, started the engine, and pulled away, rambling on down the old country road. The moment the car disappeared around a corner, the rain started again. First a drizzle and then a deluge. Jason didn't even have time to open his umbrella.

He dragged himself into his truck and glanced down at his white shirt. A streak of grease ran from his shoulder to the middle of his chest. Miss Eulalie never did care how a man looked after a long day at work. She always told him it was what was inside that counted. At times, he swore she could look inside him and see the anger and the grief that had driven him out of New York.

He held the coin out to stare at it, tilting it from one side to the other. He recognized the profile of Julius Caesar. This coin was very old, but in mint condition. Where had the old man found such a prize? Jason couldn't believe he'd let Mr. Cupidano talk him into accepting it.

He started the engine. Now he would really be late for Miss Eulalie's funeral, but she would be the first one to understand. Miss Eulalie never turned down a person in need, especially one Jason Stavros.

***

Cupid stepped on the gas. His old car rose into the air, transforming into a chariot pulled by four winged stallions. The chariot rose high into the sky until the storm clouds were left behind and the sun warmed his face.

Venus metamorphosed from a shriveled old woman to her normal, breathtakingly beautiful self. Her gray hair turned black and fell from the confining bun to stream about her shoulders like a cascade of water, bubbling and alive. "Oh, I thought I was going suffocate in those horrible shoes. Why do women wear things that are so enclosed?" She held her foot out, wiggling red-painted toenails. "You can't show off your pedicure."

Cupid rolled his eyes. She was at it again, totally absorbed in herself. "Ma, I don't want to hear about your toes. You were flirting with that man."

She shrugged. "So what. I'm allowed. I'm the Goddess of Love. That's who I am. That's what I do."

"Haven't you learned your lesson about mortals? Look at what happened with you, Adonis and Proserpine? The love triangle from hell."

She pouted, her bottom lip jutting out. Tears overflowed her eyes and rolled down her cheeks, turning to flowers as they fell on the bottom of the chariot. "You certainly know how to rain on a girl's parade."

The chariot soared through the sky and stopped in front of their palatial Roman mansion. Venus stepped down and stalked inside, still crying.

Cupid morphed back into cherub form and flew after her. He didn't have time for one of her temper tantrums. He was still on probation and, despite his success with his first assignment, he couldn't afford to rest on his laurels. He still needed his mom's help if he was going to regain his reputation.

"Mom," Cupid pleaded as they entered the atrium. Statues of couples clinging to each other occupied every niche. The players were in different degrees of undress. And while the faces of the men were different, the faces of the women were always the same. His mother. Venus immortalized in marble with each of her lovers. She always said her love toys rated more than just a notch on her bed post.

They moved into the salon, Cupid on his mother's heels trying to apologize. "Mom, you know I didn't mean it."

Venus sniffled. "You hurt my feelings, and you know how sensitive I am." She covered her face with her hand. Her shoulders shook. A chaise lounge slid out from the wall and positioned itself next to her as she sank gracefully onto the cushions.

Cupid sighed. What a drama queen. She only cried when she was having man problems. "Are you having trouble with Mars again?"

She sniffled. "I think he's having an affair with Pomona." Her lips quivered. "I hate that fruit tree floozy."

Cupid patted her shoulder. She became weepy and neurotic every millennia. Just like clockwork. He didn't know how to help her, and her neuroses weren't going to help him. Now that he'd given Jason the coin, he had to find Jason's soul mate.

He waved his hand and his laptop appeared, hovering in the air in front of him. "Mom," his voice was firm, "we don't have time for histrionics. You and I have a job to do."

"Okay, Cupie," she said between whimpers. "I'll try to be strong." She lifted her chin and put on her brave face. She sighed with theatrical martyrdom.

Cupid rubbed his throbbing temples. He didn't think gods had migraines, but then again he had a moody mother to contend with. "Then let's get started." He tapped a few keys on the keyboard to call up the eligible women in Jason's life. Jason's file appeared, and Cupid whistled. "Boy, his ex-wife really took him for everything he had."

Venus sniffled. "Serena is a bitch. You know hippo-faced Juno is her patron goddess." Venus inspected her fingernails. "Hate her."

A nymph appeared with a bowl of grapes and a decanter of wine. She poured wine into two golden chalices. The chalices flew through the air, one to Venus and the second to hover in the air next to Cupid. He reached out and moved it away with a glance at the nymph. She was new and apt to be over-enthusiastic. The last time she'd sent him wine, she'd spilled it all over his keyboard. The laptop was still sticky.

Cupid whistled. "No wonder this guy is so wary of women." He tapped a few more keys. "He needs a woman who is loyal, trustworthy, faithful and will love him unconditionally."

Venus shrugged. "Get him a dog."

Cupid pushed a few keys, and a dog's face appeared on his computer screen. "He already has a dog."

"I could turn Pomona into a dog. Something with a flat face that drools a lot. What do you think?

"Focus." Cupid snapped his fingers in front of her face. "Jason... Love... Saving my behind."

Venus glared at him. "Jason–-soul mate. Pomona—Bitch. I can compartmentalize. I'm with it. And I do the finger snapping around here."

Excuse me, Queen Bee. Oh, his headache was getting worse. "I need a vacation."

"Whom do you have in your date...dote...data...thingy?" She waved her hands at the computer.

"Lap-top-com-put-er," Cupid said slowly.

"Whatever."

Cupid stared at the screen again. "Jason is going to be a hard one."

"Well, just don't fix him up with someone too homely. I'd like him to have someone with breeding and class."

"Whom do you have in mind?"

"Why not Merrill Prescott the Fourth, you know, Miss Eulalie's lawyer. She is so refined and mannerly, the epitome of Southern style and grace. Her family goes back all the way to the Etruscans. Too bad about her parents, though. They were such difficult people. We never did get them to the altar. Like a hippie bonding ceremony really counts on the score card."

Cupid ignored his mother's verbal rambling. He did a file search for Merrill. At least her parents were still living together. Didn't that constitute a common-law marriage? "I like Merrill, too." But Merrill was almost too good. Harvard Law School. Straight A student. "Maybe Jason needs someone a little less over-achieving and little more blue-collar like himself. Maybe I can find him a nice waitress."

"Nonsense, Cupie dear." She snapped her fingers, and a portal opened on the floor. "We've had this argument before. And you know I'm always right."

The scene before them showed Merrill Prescott with Miss Eulalie's dog, Merrill's grandmother, and the preacher. Behind them stood Miss Eulalie's ancient butler, elderly maid and almost-blind cook. Not one of them a blood relative, but they were the only people to attend Miss Eulalie's funeral—standing in the pouring rain, heads bowed, clothes drenched despite huge umbrellas. Cupid wanted to cry. Miss 'E' had been one of his favorite mortals. She'd been tough and strong and filled with spirit. He would miss her.

Poor Jason wasn't going to make the funeral, and Cupid felt a little sad they'd delayed him. Jason had been deeply attached to Miss Eulalie. And if Venus wanted Merrill for him, Jason was going to have to come up with an excuse for missing the funeral before their relationship ever had a chance to get off the ground. According to his Oracle, Jason and Merrill weren't fated to be together. Unless....

Venus frowned briefly. "Will you look at that." Her voice grew angry. "Miss Eulalie's relatives have been waiting for her to croak for twenty years, and not one of them had the decency to show their faces at her funeral. I'll wager my last dinar they'll be at the reading of the will." She snapped her fingers. "I don't understand why Miss Eulalie left them anything at all. She was just too good for the likes of them."

"But that doesn't solve the problem of Jason and Merrill." He glanced back at the computer screen. He didn't really have anybody for either of them. How had that happened?

"Don't you worry, Cupie dear."

Warily, Cupid asked, "What are you going to do, Mom?"

She gave him a mysterious smile. "Already done. Just needs a little adjustment." She snapped her fingers again and giggled. "There. All fixed. Just you wait, Cupie. Mommy's on a roll."

One

Merrill Prescott the Fourth swivelled back and forth in her chair, staring at the hand-written note lying on her desk. The note had been in an envelope addressed to her and tucked into the file folder containing Miss Eulalie Bidwell's last will and testament.

Miss Eulalie had been Merrill's first client. But more than a client, she had been a friend. Merrill had admired Miss Eulalie's fierce independence, coupled with her ribald sense of humor and sharp wit. Merrill used to feel guilty about billing Miss Eulalie for her time because she had enjoyed the old woman's company so much. Her life wasn't going to be the same with Miss Eulalie gone.

She read the note again, still unable to believe the contents. She had no doubt of the authenticity since she recognized Miss Eulalie's unique, flowing handwriting. The date of the notary at the bottom indicated that wily Miss Eulalie had been planning her bombshell for a long time.

"Merrill, you are a woman of honor and I trust you to follow my last wishes. I didn't want to give you a chance of talking me out of my decision, hence this hand-written note. You will notice the Notary's stamp and signature to attest to its legitimacy.

'Addendum 1: Being of sound mind, I, Eulalie Hermione Whitney Bidwell, wish to make a change to my will regarding the custody of my beloved Psyche's Folly.

'I want Jason to understand, I'm not doing this because I don't trust him. Jason is not only a brilliant contractor, but has been a good friend and companion to me and my dog. But I believe my dog needs both a mother and a father. I wish Merrill Evelyn Prescott, IV, and Jason Michael Stavros to share custody of Psyche's Folly instead of Mr. Stavros acting as sole custodian. I further stipulate that both humans and dog are to reside in either of my two homes, providing a stable home life for my beloved Psyche's Folly.

'Addendum 2: I also specify that ten million dollars be set aside to create a shelter for the stray and destitute dogs of Charleston, in a manner to be determined by Merrill Prescott and Jason Stavros. They understand my feelings about stray animals and will keep them in comfort while attempting to find good, decent homes for them."

While Merrill had agreed to act as co-executor to protect Miss Eulalie's interests, playing house with Jason Stavros had not been part of the discussion. And yet, here it was in black and white. She and Jason Stavros, a man she'd never even met, were required by the terms of the will to live together in either Miss Eulalie's city home or her country estate sharing joint custody and the care and feeding of Miss Eulalie's dog.

Merrill had agreed to oversee the handling of the money, but she had not agreed to be the dog's executer. When had the old lady changed the will? Originally, Miss Eulalie had left her famous Grand Champion Kerry Blue Terrier, Psyche's Folly, in the sole custody of Jason Stavros.

Merrill could see it now. CNN and ABC were going to come knocking on the door for interviews, determined to create a sound bite. Each report would decide Miss Eulalie was crazy as a loon. Who left $75 million dollars to a dog? But then again, none of the reporters had met Miss Eulalie's niece and nephew. Those two were pieces of work. The kindest thing Merrill could say about either one of them was that they were able to color-coordinate their clothes. Other than that, good manners dictated she say nothing.

Miss Eulalie had left each one a small inheritance. Merrill knew they weren't going to be happy when they heard how very small it was. For years those two had nickled and dimed Miss Eulalie. Now she'd denied them the big score.

A knock sounded on the door, and Merrill's secretary, Lula Parsons, entered. Lula slammed the door behind her and leaned back against it, one hand pressed tight to her chest and the other fanning her face. "Lordy, Miss Prescott. If the finest piece of man flesh didn't just walk into your office. What did you do to deserve all this good fortune?"

Lula was forty-five years old and had her pale-brown hair teased to the height of the Eiffel Tower. She wore a plain blue skirt and a white blouse with a sailor collar and red bow tied under her chin.

"What does he want?" Merrill asked.

Lula clutched her neck. "Who can pay attention to what a man who looks like he does says?"

Merrill frowned. "Then you find out, and don't come back until you do. I have Miss Eulalie's relatives coming soon for the reading of the will."

Lula nodded. She backed out the door and seconds later returned, a blush on her pale cheeks. "He says that's what he's here for—the reading of the will."

"The vultures commeth."

"He says he's not related to Miss Eulalie. He says he's her carpenter, Jason Stavros."

Merrill looked at the will. Jason Stavros! The man she was supposed to live with until Psyche's Folly followed her mistress into the great beyond. He hadn't attended the funeral either. He was probably just like Miss Eulalie's relatives—just in it for the money.

Merrill took a deep breath. She took a second to get her game face on. "Show Mr. Stavros in."

Lula fanned her face. "Get out your asbestos undies, Boss. You're goin' to need them." She laughed, a great cackling sound that reminded Merrill of a crow on helium.

Merrill sat back in her leather chair and straightened the lapels on her still damp black silk jacket. When she felt ready, she nodded to Lula, who opened the door and motioned for the man to enter. "Mr. Stavros, Miss Prescott will see you now."

Jason Stavros strolled in, his muscular shoulders filling the doorway. Merrill bit her bottom lip. My God. He was a five alarm fire. Asbestos undies weren't enough. He smiled, giving his squarish face an almost boyish quality. Her stomach clenched. The *lusties* were *not* on her agenda.

She continued to survey. His aquiline nose had been broken and was now slightly crooked, just enough of a flaw to make everything else seem perfect. His black hair was a little long, but he was the consummate specimen of tall, dark, and delectable manhood. She had not dated in a long time, and sharing the dog with him was going to stretch her self-control to the limit.

Switching her attention from his face to his body, she noted that his pants and shirt clung damply, showing off the rugged quality of his physique. He held his suit jacket over his arm. A streak of dirt decorated the pristine whiteness of his shirt, the bare tanned forearm, and his cheek. For a construction worker, he dressed well. He looked good, too. Lula had not exaggerated.

Merrill's throat went dry. She rose, and held out her hand. "Mr. Stavros. How nice to meet you."

He spread his hands to show the dirt. "Thanks, Miss Prescott. Sorry, but my hands are dirty. In fact, I'm dirty."

She steeled herself, determined not to be distracted by his oh so attractive face. "Whatever happened, Mr. Stavros? I was expecting you at the funeral." She was glad he'd been late. He would have been too much of a diversion to mourn properly, although she knew Miss Eulalie would have forgiven her the impure thoughts. She had remarked on numerous occasions that mold had a more exciting love life than Merrill.

He hung his jacket on the back of a chair. "This elderly couple had a flat tire, and I stopped to change it. By the time I arrived at the cemetery, the ceremony was over and everyone had left. I'm sorry I missed it. I liked Eulalie. Missing her funeral seems disrespectful."

He didn't have the air of a white knight about him. In fact, he reminded her of a swashbuckling pirate. "It's lucky for them you came along. Are William Poundstone and the ladies with you?"

He smiled. "Mabel wasn't feeling well, and they're all still grieving. Since Miss Eulalie already told them what is in the will for them, I insisted they stay home."

Not only was that sensible, but that was very compassionate of him. Why drag them out in the rain again when they already knew what Miss Eulalie had left them? "Then won't you sit down while we wait for the others? May I offer you coffee, or tea?" *Or me*, she thought, and then chastised herself. What was wrong with her? She never had these kinds of thoughts. Especially since this man was now her client.

"Water will be fine, and a place to wash up, if I may." He glanced ruefully at the smear of dirt across his chest.

Merrill pointed him toward the door of her executive washroom. He thanked her and closed the door. She heard the sound of water running. She sighed, imagining him washing his long, slender fingers. He had beautiful hands. She could just imagine the talents that those fingers had. She shook her head, trying to bring her errant thoughts back into control. She felt as though someone had cast a spell over her. A love spell.

How ridiculous.

Lula knocked and entered. She rolled her eyes. "Didn't I tell you, Boss? Hot hunk of burning love. You better jump on that. You're not getting any younger."

"Lula," she stage-whispered and pointed at the bathroom. "He's in there."

Lula leaned forward. "Then go in there and see if he needs any help washing his hands."

"What do you want, Lula?" Merrill said, scowling.

"Guess who's here? The dumb and the desperate." She jerked her thumb back at the door to the reception area.

Lula had no more use for Belle Boyd Bidwell Beaumont and Jefferson Davis Bidwell than Miss Eulalie had. Merrill took a deep breath, girding herself for the coming histrionics when they found out what was in the will.

Jefferson Davis Butler Bidwell bopped into her office like he was dancing on a cloud. His tall, thin body shook with suppressed excitement. Merrill swore he mouthed the word "Jackpot" as he sat his Armani-covered derriere on her chair. He smiled at her while pushing his hand through a patch of thinning blond hair.

Merrill wanted to slap the silly grin off his face. He had the manners of a gentleman, but the personality of a slug.

"Miss Prescott." His voice held a supercilious note, a sense of entitlement that left Merrill with a nagging sense of distaste. "Forgive me for being late for my great aunt's funeral, but I had an unexpected business matter to deal with."

Right. Merrill wondered if he was paying off his bookie, his loan shark, or one of the downtown tarts he called a girlfriend. J.D. Bidwell dressed and acted like old Southern quality, but the truth was, the man liked to wallow in the mud just like every other pig.

J.D.'s sister, Belle Boyd Bidwell Beaumont, floated into the room. Her yellow chiffon dress billowed around her. The huge, floppy brim of her hat bobbed. She was the ideal of the Southern belle fifty years too late. Her expensively tinted blonde hair was pulled back into a loose chignon at the nape of her neck. "Hello, Miss Prescott. Such a dreary day, isn't it?" She offered Merrill a handshake with a surprisingly strong grip. "How are you? Sorry, Henry and I couldn't attend the funeral. His asthma, you know. He just couldn't breathe." She glanced back at her husband.

Henry Beaumont was a hunched over, colorless man, twenty years older then Belle. He faded more with each passing year. Merrill thought, if left alone, he would eventually disappear into transparent nothingness. Belle's use for him was quickly coming to an end. She was in the market for hot new blood, which reminded Merrill of Jason Stavros still washing up in her bathroom.

As though thought precipitated action, the bathroom door swung open, and Jason stepped out, looking clean and virile. His hands were scrubbed, and the smear of grease on his face had been removed. He glanced at J.D. and Belle Boyd. "I see the siblings have arrived. Hi, J.D. Hi, there, Belle. Nice dress. Did you buy it for the funeral?"

Belle glared at him. "Mr. Stavros, I didn't think you were concerned about my fashion choices."

Merrill glanced sharply at Belle Boyd. Miss Eulalie had often complained about Belle's voracious appetites. Once, Miss Eulalie had told Merrill that Belle had tried to seduce Jason and, according to Miss Eulalie, she and Jason had laughed for weeks over Belle's behavior. Merrill didn't know any man who had ever turned down Belle Boyd. Miss Eulalie had once remarked that Belle was the most visited tourist trap in Charleston.

"What is he doin' here?" J.D. burst out angrily, pointing at Jason. His finger shook with indignation. "I demand to know why this...this...handyman is here."

Merrill forced herself not to smile. There was not a lot of love in this room. Wait until she dropped the bomb. "Mr. Stavros is mentioned in the will."

Belle sighed, a dramatic hand against her forehead. "Miss Eulalie always had a soft spot in her heart for her *servants*. Any hard luck story...." Her voice trailed away as though she had no energy to continue. A wan, patronizing smile crossed her lips.

Jason grinned. "I do try my best, Miss Belle." He walked to the back of the room and leaned on the paneled wall, crossing one foot over the other at the ankle.

"I wouldn't know about that." Belle sank gracefully into a chair. She pointed at the chair behind her, and her husband obediently fell into it.

Merrill sat down behind her large desk and picked up Miss Eulalie's will. She wasn't going to get through this reading without bloodshed. "Shall we get started? I have two documents here. The original will, and a hand-written, notarized letter from Miss Eulalie. I'll read the original will first, and then the handwritten one."

Jason moved to a chair, sat down, and stretched out his long legs. J.D. lounged against the fireplace, one arm resting on the mantle in his best Rhett Butler imitation pose. He drew a gold cigarette case out of his inner pocket and popped it open, a brown cigarillo appearing between his fingers. He tapped the cigarette on the gold cigarette case.

"Not in my office, Mr. Bidwell," Merrill said sternly. She showed him the plaque hanging on the wall next to him, announcing that her office was a no smoking zone.

"Well, *excu-use* me, Miss Prescott." He returned the cigarillo back to his ornately engraved gold case and stuck his bottom lip out like a two-year-old.

Lula slipped into the office and sat in the back corner. She wore a maniacal grin. Even Merrill couldn't keep her own amusement from bubbling over. Belle Boyd and J.D. were in for one heck of a surprise.

Merrill opened the original will. "I Miss Eulal—."

"Excuse me, Miss Prescott," Belle interrupted with a languid wave of her hand. "Skip the formalities. I have to get my Henry home and see that he is properly medicated. I can hear him wheezing."

Merrill studied Henry. He was sound asleep in the chair, totally oblivious to his surroundings. As if on cue, a tiny snore erupted from his drooping lips.

Merrill snuck a peek at Jason Stavros. He removed his tie and unbuttoned his shirt. Just one more button. His skin was golden. Merrill held her breath, wondering if his skin was smooth. She could just imagine what he looked like without his clothes. Heat rose in her, fanning outward like a tidal wave. She could barely catch her breath. She gave herself a mental shake. *Get your mind back on business.*

"Very well, then," Merrill continued, "I'll get to the meat. 'I, Eulalie Hermione Whitney Bidwell leave to my trusted servants, Ruby S. Jackson, William A. Poundstone, and Mabel Lee Turner, two million dollars each and give them permission to continue living in either of my two homes as long as they wish.'"

Belle fidgeted. She kept glancing at her brother, a frown creasing her forehead. If she wasn't careful, she'd get wrinkles.

"'To my niece,'" Merrill said, "'Belle Boyd Bidwell Beaumont, and my nephew, Jefferson Davis Bidwell....'" Merrill's voice trailed off. She was a coward. She didn't want to read the rest, but a glance at Jason gave her courage. He smiled at her and nodded. She knew if anyone attacked, he'd protect her.

Belle sat up straight, tugging her hem down over her slender calves. J.D. left off lounging on the mantle to move tensely toward his sister. He gripped her hand.

Merrill swallowed and went on, "'...I leave the sum of two hundred and fifty thousand dollars to each.'"

"What?" Belle gasped and jumped to her feet. "What did you say?" She stood poised on the balls of her feet, one hand wrapped around her throat, the other clenched in a tight fist. "Repeat what you just said. I don't think you have it right."

Merrill repeated the provision. The wording hadn't changed. Belle went red, then white, then red again. J.D. gasped like a fish sucking in fresh air. His blue eyes bulged out of his head.

"You must be mistaken." Belle fanned her face furiously with her hand. "My aunt," Belle squeaked, "would not leave more money to her servants than to us, her own family, her flesh and blood."

"Please sit down, Mrs. Beaumont." Merrill took a deep breath. The best was yet to come. "I haven't finished reading the will."

J.D. solicitously helped his sister back into the chair. "Two hundred fifty thousand dollars? She only left me two hundred fifty thousand dollars. Why that old...." His sister elbowed him in the side. J.D. seemed to take stock of himself, and he bit his lips. "What happened to the seventy-five million dollars my aunt was worth?"

"I'm getting to that." Merrill glanced at Jason, who held his side, laughing as silently as he could. Another button had popped open, revealing even more of the golden skin of his chest. For a moment, Merrill forgot to breathe.

A small chuckle escaped Jason, and Belle turned to frown angrily at him. "This isn't funny, Mr. Stavros." She sank back into her chair, a little squeaky breath whooshing out of her.

Merrill could tell Jason Stavros was having a good time, and that he had no idea what was coming next. She took a deep breath. "'To my beloved dog, Psyche's Folly,'" Merrill continued, "'I leave the bulk of my estate.'"

Belle jumped to her feet again, wailing. J.D. shook his fist. "The dog! You can't mean that damn dog gets all *my* money?"

Merrill shrugged. "That's what the will says."

"That dog!" Belle screeched. "That dog!"

Merrill resisted the impulse to cover her ears. "Please sit down, Mrs. Beaumont. There is more."

"More?" Belle broke into wild laughter. "More what? More humiliation? Another stab in the back from that old bitch? I spent the best years of my life being nice to that old biddy, and that's how she repays me?"

"Mrs. Beaumont." Merrill pointed at the chair. "Sit down. Now!"

The other woman fell back into the chair. A loud sniff escaped her thin lips.

Merrill glanced over to Belle's sleeping husband. He hadn't moved an inch. He seemed totally oblivious to the hurricane brewing. She wondered if he was still among the living.

J.D. cleared his throat. "Who is to administer all this for the dog?"

Belle sat up and smiled. "Of course, our dear Aunt Eulalie wouldn't leave her beloved Polly to some stranger."

Merrill nodded. "You do mean Psyche's Folly, don't you?

"Of course," Belle said with a little blush.

Merrill said, "You're quite right, your aunt does not intend to leave her beloved dog to strangers."

Belle's smile widened as she patted her brother on the hand, a hopeful glint sparkling in her eyes. She hadn't given up yet.

J.D. leaned forward, his patronizing smile back on his face. "Which one of us gets the dog? Belle or I?"

Merrill just loved dropping bombshells. Then there were days like this, when she could unload her entire arsenal. "I'm afraid it's a joint custody. In her hand-written addendum, Miss Eulalie states that–"

"We both share custody?" Belle examined her nails, preening once more. "I can live with that."

"Not exactly." Merrill twisted the note, preparing herself for the next outburst. She cleared her throat and quickly read the first addendum, girding herself for the thunderstorm to come.

Belle screamed. "No!" She covered her face and broke into loud, hysterical tears.

Henry finally woke up, blinking. "What's wrong, dearest?"

"Shut up, Henry. Did you hear that?" Belle wailed. "J.D., you make her tell us the truth. Aunt Eulalie would never leave her sweet, adorable dog to strangers. I love that critter. And little Molly loves me."

Merrill set the will down and studied Belle. "I am telling the truth. Here's her notarized note." She looked at Jason. He leaned forward and took the paper off the desk, frowning. Merrill noticed how strong and powerful his hand was. A shimmer of desire drifted over her body. She felt herself flush. Here she was, two hours after the funeral of one of her best friends, and she was hot to trot with some man she had just met.

Jason smiled at her as though he knew what she was thinking. Mortified, she stared down at her desk. She couldn't get involved with someone who was essentially a client, not withstanding the fact that she didn't really trust him any more than she did Belle or J. D. He had his own angle, despite his story about missing Miss Eulalie's funeral.

His eyes were dark and mysterious. Merrill had no clue what he was thinking or what he was feeling. He kept his face calm and in control, though a little muscle at the side of his mouth quirked.

J.D. jumped to his feet, his chair sliding back and bumping against the wall with the force of his movement. "I don't understand. Aunt Eulalie loved me. She would never leave her dog's welfare to a stranger."

Merrill smiled sweetly. "What makes you think Mr. Stavros and I are strangers?"

Belle twisted around in her seat to glare at Jason. She pointed a pink acrylic fingernail at him. "He's not one of us. He's a confidence man out to cheat J.D. and me out of what's rightfully ours. That dog's family. I love it more than I love my husband."

Why am I not surprised at that? The dog came with a bank account, and Henry was tapped out. *Poor Henry,* Merrill thought, *his usefulness has ended.*

"I'll have the will voided and nullified," J.D. cried.

"On what grounds?" Merrill inquired.

J.D. replied, "That old woman was crazy. She didn't have the sense to know what she was doing."

"Would you care to explain that to me?"

"My aunt would never leave her precious Trolley to you or to that *janitor.*" He made janitor sound like a dirty word as he shook a finger at Jason. "She wasn't right in her head. I believe you beguiled her, Miss Prescott. Both of you beguiled her. You turned her against Belle and me."

Merrill cringed. They spoke like characters in a bad Tennessee Williams play.

She rose to her feet. "Mr. Bidwell, if you believe either Mr. Stavros or I acted improperly, then you are well within your rights to file a complaint with the proper authority. If you believe Miss Eulalie's will is invalid, you do have legal recourse. But if you cast aspersions on my behavior, I warn you now, I'll turn this into a dog fight, excuse my metaphor."

Belle Boyd squeezed her brother's arm. "What happens to the money when the dog dies?"

They weren't going to like what Merrill had to say next. "Once Psyche's Folly is deceased, the money is to be set up in a trust fund designed to benefit both public and private animal shelters throughout the state. Also, Mr. Stavros and I are authorized to immediately set aside ten million dollars for a private shelter to be administered by us."

"And," Belle continued, "who will decide which shelter is funded once the beast is dead?"

"Mr. Stavros and I will continue to have full discretion over how the money is distributed."

J.D. looked as though he would choke. "Under those circumstances, we will see you in court, you shyster." He turned and tried to storm away.

Jason jumped up and grabbed J.D. by the arm. "You apologize to Miss Prescott."

J.D. stared at Jason's hand, tightly gripping his arm just above the elbow. "I will not." He tried to yank himself free.

"Apologize." Jason's voice was tense. "You're going to have a hard time spending your money while you're in traction."

J.D. squared his sloped shoulders and glanced back at Merrill. "I apologize."

Merrill simply nodded.

Belle gripped the arms of the chair. "This is all a joke, right?" She laughed nervously. "Miss Eulalie always had a fine sense of humor. One time, she even left us in Nashville. Told us to take the bus home. Ha! Ha!"

"Mrs. Beaumont," Merrill said, "this isn't a joke. Though a few details need to be worked out, we are finished here."

Belle started for the door. Lula jumped up, opened it and stood to one side. "Bye, y'all. Have a nice day. Come back real soon, now, ya hear."

When Belle and J.D. had left, still angrily trying to figure out what to do, Lula slammed the door after them and leaned against it, laughing so hard she doubled over. "Boss, that was a hoot and a half."

"Thank you, Lula. If you would please...." Merrill gestured for Lula to leave. "I have some things to talk over with Mr. Stavros."

"Don't you need me to take notes? Dictation?"

"No, Lula."

Lula leaned forward. "Are ya sure?"

"Yes, Lula. I'm sure. And when you're outside, no eavesdropping."

Lula grimaced but made a graceful exit.

Alone with Jason Stavros, Merrill sank back into her chair, relieved at having Miss Eulalie's relatives gone. "Mr. Stavros." She stopped and just stared at him. Even her feet got excited looking at him. She hoped she wasn't perspiring.

He smiled and took the seat opposite her. "Jason, please."

Merrill wet her lips. "We need to talk about our situation."

"I do better talking about 'situations' over lunch."

A restaurant was a nice, public place. She'd be able to act normally. She stood and grabbed her umbrella. "Let's have lunch.

***

Jupiter sat on his throne drumming his fingers. He fought a yawn as Sigmund Freud paced back and forth in front of him. Jupiter cast a sideways glance at his wife, Juno, disliking her for insisting they attend couple's therapy. He didn't need therapy. So what if he had a roaming eye and roving hands? He always came back to her.

Sexual conquests were just a hobby. He had a hard job, dealt with a lot of stress, and he occasionally needed relief.

His gaze wandered away from Siggy. He tuned out the drone of psycho-babble that kept Juno totally occupied. To one side where she couldn't see, Jupiter opened a portal on the meeting room to check on what his fellow gods were up to. Just because he was in therapy didn't mean he could ignore his responsibilities.

Discordia was traveling with a heavy metal rock band. Apollo was in the act of seducing a water nymph in his hot tub. Minerva hunched over her scrolls again. Dull girl. She intended to record the history of the universe. Jupiter couldn't believe she was his daughter. The thought of her still gave him a headache. He searched for Venus and Cupid, his favorites. They understood him and never became angry because he liked his fun on the side.

Venus was in her mansion, a portal to the mortal world open on her floor. Cupid hovered over her, his little wings beating hard against the air. The window showed a woman and a dog. The woman was beautiful.

Jupiter clutched his chest. Flowing blonde hair framed a perfect oval face. Green eyes, the color of the spring fields outside Tuscany, dominated her face. Her body was slender, yet rounded in all the right, womanly places. She was take-his-breath-away beautiful.

Jupiter felt a stirring in him. He had to have her.

Wait a minute! What was Venus and Cupid's interest in this woman? Of course, they were trying to match her up.

No! No! No! No! Dibs on the mortal, he wanted to scream. He stroked his long white beard, wondering how to distract Venus and Cupid from interfering in his soon-to-be love life.

An idea popped into his head. He turned the idea around, trying to find a flaw. None occurred to him. Of course, nothing was wrong with his plan. It was his plan. Oh, he was good. He was really good. He had to go find some nymph to pat him on the back.

"Juno," he said. "My love."

Juno smiled at him. "Yes, my darling husband."

"I have some urgent business to attend to." He snapped his fingers and disappeared.

Two

The rain had cleared, and the sun peeked through the clouds. Jason took Merrill to the Courtyard Tavern. The waiter seated them near the fountain. A beam of sunlight shimmered on her hair. Despite the rising heat, she looked cool and elegant in her black suit, and yet she had a seductive, earthy quality about her that never overshadowed her aristocratic presence.

"We appear to have something of a dilemma." Merrill smoothed her napkin over her lap.

Her words startled him out of his reverie. For a long moment, he'd forgotten she was a lawyer and that he didn't like lawyers. "I don't get it. What dilemma?"

Merrill stared at the menu. "There is no way I can share custody with you. The dog can't possibly live in my house."

He seemed surprised. "You don't like dogs?"

"I like dogs just fine, although I've never owned a pet. I've always lived with my grandmother, and she is deathly allergic to dogs and cats."

"No problem. You can live at Eulalie's."

"That poses too many complications."

He shrugged. "Because of the construction? Most of the renovation is complete. All I have left are a few projects on the ground floor."

"Let me see how I can put this delicately." She rubbed her forehead, and then looked him straight in the eye. "Where do you sleep?"

His stomach clenched. He knew where he'd like to be sleeping—in a big brass bed with her tucked up close to him, her butt against his... *Shut up, Stavros. You're getting yourself all worked up, and you haven't even gotten to the main course yet.* He took a huge gulp of water. He'd love to wake up next to her each morning. Her hair would be all tousled, falling around her shoulders, and her eyes would be dreamy with sleep. Just the thought of being so close to her got him all fired up.

Merrill snapped her fingers in front of his face. "Mr. Stavros, would you please concentrate on our conversation?"

Good idea, Stavros. Stop looking at her. Stop daydreaming about her. Concentrate on the problem at hand. Not on the babe. "Where I always sleep. In the guest house. It's big enough for me and Buster."

"Buster?"

"My dog." Buster was his best friend. They'd been together for years.

"You have a dog, too?"

Buster had seen him through the hell he'd called marriage and the inferno of his divorce. "Where Buster goes, I go."

Merrill nodded. "Of course, Mr. Stavros."

"Excuse me. Remember, I said call me Jason."

The waiter had been hovering over them for nearly five minutes. The courtyard was filling up with other diners. They ordered.

"What's wrong with living at Eulalie's?" Jason queried when the waiter had departed.

"I wasn't prepared for this situation."

He frowned at her. "What's to prepare?"

"Did you know Miss Eulalie had added that last provision about me sharing custody with you?"

He was surprised. "You mean you didn't know? I thought you were her lawyer."

She frowned and shook her head. "I don't know how the change was made, or even how it got into my files. I spoke to Lula, and she says she didn't put the note there."

"Eulalie always was a slick one." He was going to miss that old lady. She'd turned his life around. He had to appreciate her tenacity. She'd told him he needed a wife, and he wondered if the extra provision was her way of trying to help him. Though, of all people, she should know that he wouldn't pick someone like Merrill Prescott. Maybe having her live at Eulalie's wasn't such a good idea. He'd married a blue-blooded beauty before, and all that had gotten him was bankruptcy and a broken heart. He wasn't dumb enough to fall for that kind of woman again, no matter how beautiful she might be, or how she affected him.

She took a deep breath and said, "My moving into Miss Eulalie's house won't appear proper."

"Proper." She sounded like a nineteenth century heroine out of a chick novel.

She folded her hands together and rested them on the table. "You misunderstand. My grandmother has lived in Charleston all her life. She has an over-developed sense of propriety. Nana never says, does, or thinks anything without considering the ramifications of her social set. And Charleston society is as tightly laced as Scarlet O'Hara's corset."

Jason broke out laughing. "That's ridiculous. This isn't the Civil War."

"Do you mean the War of Northern Aggression?"

Oops! He'd forgotten the war was still being fought in the South. "That conflict has been over for a long time."

"I know that. You know that. But as far as my grandmother is concerned, the South is still waiting for supplies. That is the attitude I have to put up with. I hope you understand why I can't live at Miss Eulalie's with you."

So it wasn't personal. He had to admire that she cared about what her grandmother thought. Being Greek, he had grown up with that same attitude. If he wasn't perfect, he would have shamed the entire family all the way back to Zeus and Aphrodite. His family was still reeling from his divorce.

"There has to be a way around this," he said. "With me in the guest house and you in the main house, I don't see a problem. Besides, there are the servants." Admittedly, except for William, they were gone. The two ladies were leaving in the morning to visit relatives and would be gone for several weeks.

"You're poking fun at me. You make me sound like an old maid. I'm a modern woman, but I have to respect my grandmother's beliefs and feelings."

He grinned. "No man could ever make fun of you. Trust me, you'll be adequately chaperoned. We'll have the dogs to watch over us. Psycho is a great chaperone. She is one dog who knows all about propriety."

"Psycho. You call Miss Eulalie's grand champion Kerry Blue Terrier, Psycho?"

"Sure. She's a little high strung, but okay. Once I took a shower with her, and we had water everywhere."

"Oh my!" A dreamy look crossed her face.

He wondered what she was thinking. He knew what he was thinking. He didn't want to repeat the shower scene with Psycho, but he wouldn't mind Merrill as a partner. The thought of water sluicing off her creamy white skin sent shivers right down to his core. This babe could raise the dead.

He waved his hand. "I'm going to let you in on a little secret about Eulalie." He leaned forward, a confidential look on his face. "Beneath all those starched crinolines, Eulalie was one hell of a woman. She drank beer, watched football, and could swear better than most construction workers I know. No matter what her nephew, Jefferson Davis says, Eulalie had all her marbles in her head and a few of everyone else's."

Merrill drummed her fingers on the table. "Leaving seventy-five million dollars to a dog is bizarre."

"Do you think Eulalie should have left everything to Tweedledumb and Tweedledumber?"

"To be honest, I would have burned my money before I left it to them."

"Exactly." At least they agreed on one thing. "So what do you think you should do?"

She shook her head. "I will not let that wonderful, vivacious woman's memory be besmirched by any hint of insanity. I will fight tooth and nail to protect her memory."

Jason smiled at her. "The only way you can do that is to follow the request in her will. And to do that, we have to live together."

Her shoulders slumped. "I know you're right."

He'd won the argument. He didn't think too many people ever won arguments against her. He'd liked the way she'd handled Belle and J.D. Merrill had backbone, and he thought she could be a wily opponent. He smiled at her. "I'll be on my best behavior."

Merrill didn't return his smile. "Do not trifle with me, Stavros."

Alarm bells went off in his head. Now that he had her at the house, what was he going to do about this unexplained physical attraction he was developing for her?

Miss Eulalie, what did you get me into?

***

Jason pulled into the driveway of Eulalie's 1840 mansion. The huge house overlooked White Point Gardens and the Atlantic Ocean beyond. She had once told him White Point Gardens was the most romantic place in the city.

He was going to miss Eulalie. She knew so much about Charleston and what made the city tick. Her little bits of gossip had entertained him on many a cozy evening in front of the fireplace with brandy snifters in hand and the dogs at their feet. Would he be doing the same with Merrill? He tried to imagine her sitting in Miss

Eulalie's favorite chair. Miss Eulalie always wore her flannel nightgown and robe, but he imagined Merrill in a black lace teddy. Sweat broke out on his upper lip.

Merrill Prescott the Fourth was one hot babe. He hadn't expected to be confronted by a luscious lady lawyer, or feel such desire for her. He should have been grieving over Eulalie's death, not getting turned on by a legal shark.

Besides, he couldn't like Merrill Prescott. She was a lawyer. It didn't matter that she'd been hired to protect Eulalie's and Psycho's interests. He still hated lawyers. After his divorce, he'd packed his truck with everything left to him after his wife's rapacious pack of shysters had practically stripped him naked.

Serena had turned so vicious he couldn't understand how he could have once loved her, or what he'd done to her to earn such rage. If not for Eulalie taking him in after his truck had broken down, he would still be roaming the country trying to figure out what had gone wrong with his marriage and his life.

He parked the truck in the garage, next to Eulalie's 1930 Rolls Royce. He patted the car. Eulalie had given him a place to heal and a place to call home. And he'd always appreciate it. He couldn't love her more if she were family.

His apartment was the second floor of the garage. He tramped up the stairs. The dogs lay in the middle of the living room floor, curled around each other. Buster, mutt extraordinaire, opened his eyes but didn't move. Psycho barely acknowledged Jason's presence. Since Miss Eulalie's death, the terrier grieved. She rarely ate and refused to play. Sometimes her mournful eyes followed Jason wherever he went, as though she was afraid of what might happen next.

Jason stopped and patted her head. "I'm not going to let anything happen to you. I promise."

She licked his fingers and dropped her head back against Buster's chest.

They all owed Eulalie a debt. He had been her all-purpose handyman, and she encouraged him to put his business back together.

Charleston was a prime place for someone like Jason. The buildings were old and always in need of specialized repair. She had insisted Jason study the guidelines the Historical Preservation Society had set up for the restoration of historic homes and, when he was ready, she let him practice on her home.

Jason loved Eulalie's mansion, though she had let things slip the last few years as she'd aged. When she'd taken Jason in, she'd given him the task of putting it all back together again. Especially when she realized she was going to die. William and the girls would still need a place to call home, and Jason would be in charge of seeing to their welfare. Now that most of the work was done, he was beginning to get commissions from Eulalie's neighbors as an historical restorationist.

***

Merrill prepared for bed. For the rest of the day, her thoughts had been filled with nothing but Jason Stavros. She hadn't even talked to her grandmother yet about her situation because Merrill's grandmother preferred bad news over breakfast. Bad news over dinner kept her up all night, and if Nana was up, then Merrill was up.

She sat on the edge of the bed and massaged her feet. The clock glowed red. Nine o'clock. She seldom went to bed this early. But for the last few hours, a little voice had whispered in her head: *sleep, dream, sleep, dream.* Her eyelids felt so heavy, she could hardly keep them open. *Sleep, dream, sleep, dream.* Miss Eulalie's funeral had been harder to endure than she'd thought.

She lay back and closed her eyes. A cool night breeze caressed her cheek. She couldn't remember her bed ever being so comfortable. As she drifted, images of Jason invaded her dreams.

She opened her eyes, but she wasn't in her bedroom. She was in an old Greek temple. Jason lay on a chaise lounge, wearing a brief toga. A wreath of gold leaves encircled his head. He smiled at her.

Her feet moved her forward. She felt powerless to stop. Jason stood and winked at her. She felt a rush of silk on her skin and when she looked down, she found herself naked, a pool of white fabric at her feet.

Jason held his hand out to her, and she took it. He drew her to the lounge and gently pushed her back against the pillows. Heat flooded through her. She gasped with the intensity of her feelings for him.

He released the corner of his toga and it fell off his body, revealing his darkly tanned skin and finely etched muscles. He was beautiful. Broad shoulders tapered to a rock hard chest. A sprinkling of dark hair adorned his skin. A ripple of abdominal muscles tapered to a well-defined waist and slim, narrow hips. She stopped herself from looking down any farther. She felt a flush glow over all her body. She shouldn't be here. He was her client. What was she thinking? She could be disbarred.

"Merrill"—his voice was thick with passion—"this is a dream. We can be whoever we want to be here."

"Okay."

He laughed and lay next to her, his fingers entwining in her hair. He pulled her to him and kissed her gently. His leg slid over hers. *Oh no! I'm having a sex dream.*

"No, Merrill," he whispered in her ear. "We're making love." One hand spread over her breast.

"I could be disbarred."

He nibbled at her lips. "This is a dream. Relax. Enjoy."

"Are you sure? This feels so real."

"I'm sure. Trust me."

Her toes curled. What would one little dream hurt? She felt as though she were getting away with something really, really naughty. She smiled and gave herself up to passion.

***

Merrill sat at Blythe Prescott's massive dining table, staring at the pile of bills her grandmother had accumulated for the Fall Cotillion. Her breakfast remained uneaten at her elbow. She had put off the bills way too long. The party was less than a week away, and her grandmother buzzed around, taking care of all the last minute details with the force of a general. Nana hadn't taken on such a project for years.

Yet she couldn't focus. Her dream kept returning over and over again to haunt her. For the last ten minutes, she'd been staring at the electric bill, still not sure how much she owed the power company.

"Merrill." Her grandmother's voice seemed to come from a great distance. "You know how I feel about consuming a nutritious breakfast."

Merrill stared at the bacon. There was nothing nutritious there. "Nana, I'm still a little upset over Miss Eulalie."

Blythe Prescott was a tall, slender woman who carried herself proudly despite her seventy-eight years. Blythe was always trendy, even though she could barely afford to pay the electric bill Merrill was still pondering.

"Nana," Merrill moved from the electric bill to the estimates from the caterer. "Beluga caviar! Don't you think something a little less expensive would do as well?"

Blythe pounded her silver-headed cane on the floor. "Only beluga caviar has passed these lips, and nothing but beluga caviar ever will. I will not soil my palate with anything less. This is going to be the party to start the new millennia off on the right foot."

"The millennia doesn't begin until 2001."

Again that cane struck the floor. "I know that. Send a child to a northern college, and she comes back smart-mouthed and disrespectful."

They had this discussion all the time. Yet Blythe was the one who insisted Merrill attend the best school money could buy. Of course, she had received a full scholarship. "Nana, Harvard Law School did not teach me to be disrespectful. They taught me to be a lawyer." Being a lawyer paid the bills and kept them from being tossed out on their backsides.

Merrill sighed. She might have to reconsider her ethics and start chasing ambulances to pay for this party. The Prescott family had always been wealthy. But their money had not withstood Uncle Eli Prescott's need to show he could increase the fortune without having to go to work.

"Nana, we have to come to a compromise."

Her grandmother's gaze sharpened. "Compromise." She drew out the 'S' in a scornful hiss. "Other people compromise, Merrill. Not Prescotts."

"We are in debt above our eyeballs. The money coming to me as executer of Eulalie's estate is not going to put a nick in our debts. Mr. Jessell could have foreclosed on us years ago." She glanced around at the old room with its priceless antiques.

"Pinky would never throw us out." Her grandmother shook her head. "Our families have been friends for decades."

"Which is why he's been so lenient with us. If only you'd relent and let me sell the Louis XVI settee. You hate it."

Blythe held her hand up. "We are not going to speak about selling one stick of furniture in this house. Almost every chair and sideboard has been in the family since the first Prescott settled in Jamestown. I would part with my blood before I part with anything."

Merrill didn't need a genealogy lesson. She needed money. "You've never used that French Renaissance parlor set."

Blythe glared at her. "I will rearrange every stick of furniture in this house just to prove to you that I can't part with it."

Merrill leaned forward. "We can't even hire someone to move it."

"I will not listen to such irreverence for our way of life."

"Uncle Eli already killed our way of life. We're paupers."

Blythe clutched her heart and wheezed. "Oh my heavens. I'm palpitating. Call the doctor."

Merrill covered her face with her hands. All she asked for was one piece of furniture. One cast-off chair that had never seen the light of day would pay for this whole damned party.

Blythe sat down, waving her hand in front of her face. "I'm having a heart attack. I can't breathe."

"If you can't breathe, then how come you haven't stopped talking?"

Blythe jumped to her feet again and shook her finger at Merrill. "This is what that bohemian existence your parents insisted on living has taught you. They disregarded every tradition and value I tried to instill in them."

Merrill started laughing. If it wasn't her Northern education, then the fault lay at her parents' hippie existence. The whole scene was so ludicrous, and so typical of her grandmother. She couldn't fight it.

Blythe glared at her. "Are you finished bemoaning the state of our finances?"

"For the moment." Merrill looked away, knowing she had accomplished nothing.

Blythe picked up a little silver bell and rang it. A servant wheeled in a dress rack with several plastic shrouded gowns. "Your frocks arrived this morning."

Merrill thrust our her chin. "I don't need a new gown."

"I cannot have you looking like a ragamuffin." Blythe brushed Merrill's objection away. "This cotillion is too important for you to look like last year's designer cast-offs."

Merrill closed her eyes. "I have a gown. I can have the dressmaker put a bow or a silk flower here and there, and no one will ever know I've had it since high school."

The silver-headed cane rapped the floor again. "Merrill Evelyn Prescott the Fourth, tradition demands you have a new frock for every cotillion. That is the way it has been and always will be." She pronounced that statement with the finality of a minister ending a sermon.

"We really don't have the money, Nana." If Blythe continued to spend, Merrill would have to dip into the family trust fund again, and she hated to do that. The trust fund was enough to take care of her grandmother's everyday expenses.

"Trust me, dear, after this cotillion, we will have all the money we need." Blythe patted her hand.

Merrill's headache increased in intensity. "And, pray tell, how is the cotillion going to bring us money?" As if she didn't already know.

Blythe shook her head. "I intend to find you a proper husband." She waved the servant away, and the woman rolled the dress rack back out the door.

"Grandmother, I'm not marrying someone just because they are financially solvent."

Blythe glared at Merrill. "I did. My mama did, and my grandmother before her. Even Eulalie did."

"Eulalie loved Essex with all her heart."

Her grandmother sighed. "Merrill, women may fall in love with their husbands after marriage, but we still marry with our eyes wide open and our hearts intact. Essex Bidwell had a fine pedigree and the intelligence to find a woman who knew more about the stock market than all the brokers on Wall Street put together." Blythe took a deep breath. "I know you think I don't know what happened to our fortune, but it is our good name and your hard work that have kept a roof overhead." She curled her fingers around Merrill's. "Sugar, I don't want you working so hard. I want you to have the type of life I had. Parties and being surrounded by beautiful things." Blythe stroked her antique rosewood table. "You deserve beautiful things. If you find yourself the right man, you could have everything without lifting a finger, and all you'd have to do is smile pretty. There isn't a man in the whole South who wouldn't want to be connected to the Prescotts. Our name still counts for something. Our name brings tradition, style and influence. Why shouldn't we trade on that? It's just as easy to fall in love with a rich man as it is to fall in love with a poor man."

Merrill stared at her grandmother. Blythe was so afraid of losing everything she still had, she would do anything to preserve it. Merrill felt a deep swell of sympathy. "Nana, I promise I won't let you be thrown out on the street."

Merrill stacked the pile of bills and shoved them into a file folder. The best thing to do was take the bills to her office and figure out which ones needed to be paid now and which ones she could delay. She opened her briefcase and secured the file folder inside. She realized she hadn't told her Grandmother about Miss Eulalie's will. "Before I leave, I have to tell you about what happened at the reading yesterday."

"I shall miss Eulalie, even though she was crazy as a loon. Leaving all the money to that dog."

Merrill sighed. She could cross off Nana as a character witness on Miss Eulalie's behalf. "Miss Eulalie did what she thought was right."

"At least she didn't leave the money to her niece and nephew." Blythe shuddered. "Those children are cursed."

Merrill couldn't have agreed more. "It's about the dog."

"Didn't Eulalie leave that man custody of the dog?"

"Eulalie left custody of the dog to both me and Mr. Stavros."

Blythe looked thunderstruck. "You have to take care of the beast's needs?" Blythe frowned. "I will not have that mangy animal in my house."

"Nana, I need to go where the dog is. I'm going to have to move into Miss Eulalie's home until I can work out some sort of arrangement with Mr. Stavros."

Blythe clutched her throat. "You're going to leave me alone in this big old house? What will I do with all this space by myself."

Merrill wanted to yell, "Sell it, sell it," but wisely kept her mouth shut.

"I guess I'll have to plan the cotillion all by myself."

Merrill wasn't sure, but she thought she saw a quick smile on her grandmother's lips. "I'll still help."

Blythe shook her head. "But darlin', that would be so much extra work on your part. Don't worry yourself. I can do this."

Merrill could almost hear the little wheels spinning in Blythe's head. With no Merrill around, she could spend all the money she wanted, and Merrill wouldn't be able to stop the old girl.

Her grandmother smiled. "Don't even give me a second thought. I will be just fine. But I do expect you for Sunday dinner–every Sunday at four. And there is the phone."

She might as well get the engraver started on the wedding invitation. Merrill had the feeling she was going to get a husband whether she wanted one or not. Maybe she could run away. She started forming an escape plan.

***

Venus was so proud of herself, getting Somnus to send those erotic dreams to both Jason and Merrill. They had been terrific dreams designed to show Merrill and Jason their destinies. Paving the way, so to speak. Venus shivered with delight. Merrill Prescott was going to be a snap.

"Hey, Nessy," someone yelled.

Venus looked up and saw Proserpine enter the arena. She had chalk-white skin, glowing red eyes and straight, black hair. She wore a black leather bustier, mini-skirt and thigh-high black leather boots. The raven perched on one shoulder was a bit much. Chubby little Bacchus clung to her other hand. His grape crown dipped over his ear, and he held a gold chalice in one hand. Their affair was the hottest topic of gossip in the heavens.

Mars and Pomona walked past her. Venus tried to look away, but she couldn't take her eyes off Mars. Today he wore his bronze armor. She loved the way the breast plate fitted over his pectoral muscles. She loved the little diamond nipples. How could he wear something she had made for him, while he made time with that banana tree bimbo?

According to the rumors, Pomona was about as exciting as a mushy avocado. Venus's heart ached. She would never get over loving Mars, and it pained her to see him wasted on such geekiness.

Cupid snapped into existence in front of her face. She stared at him. He was hardly bigger than a cricket, and she wondered why he'd chosen such a miniature form.

"Whatcha doin', Ma?" he squeaked.

"I can barely hear you."

He pumped himself up until he was the size of a mouse. "What are you doing?"

She crossed her arms. "Plotting a homicide."

"You know Rule Number One: Be ruthless. Be discreet. Be lethal." He rose to flutter his wings in front of her eyes. "Is Dad after that fruit tart again?"

"Hate her," Venus replied.

A roll of thunder and a flash of lightning heralded Jupiter's appearance. He snapped into view, holding his scepter, then sat on his throne and glanced around the assembly. His face was grave with the strength of his authority.

Venus smiled and waved at him. "Hi, Daddy."

He ignored her. That shocked her. He always paid attention to her. Maybe she was losing her charm. She willed a mirror to appear and admired herself. She was perfect—as always. What could be wrong? But then a grain of suspicion worked its way to the surface. He never snubbed her like that unless he was plotting something that she wouldn't like. First, her man left her, and now her Daddy was acting suspicious. All this tension was going to give her a wrinkle! *Think happy thoughts, Venus. Happy thoughts, happy thoughts.* She could feel her upper lip twitching. *Think harder, think harder.* Oooh, her little brain hurt.

"I call this meeting to order." Jupiter's voice reverberated across the Coliseum. "By my decree." He raised his arms. "I command all gods and goddesses to immediately cease and desist with their manipulations of the human race."

Silence filled the Coliseum. Venus gulped. She glanced at Cupid, whose mouth hung open.

Bacchus stood up, his chubby little hands waving in agitation. "What about the grape harvest?"

Jupiter frowned. "The grapes will be harvested as they always are."

"But..." Bacchus squeaked.

"Silence! I have spoken." He disappeared in a puff of smoke.

For one full second silence reigned, and then everyone started yapping at once.

"Venus," Apollo yelled across the hall. "What are we going to do?"

Saturn, flinging a corner of his toga about his shoulder, clapped his hands. "Order." Everyone fell silent. He looked at Venus. "Venus, you speak to him. You're his favorite."

Gods and goddesses nodded in agreement, and Venus bit the inside of her lip. *Oh, the pressure.*

Daddy was up to no good; she could feel it right down to her sandals. First she'd get herself a facial, and then she would deal with Daddy. She had to think of something quickly. She refused to let Jupiter jeopardize her plans for Merrill and Jason.

Three

The tires of Merrill's car skidded on the wet gravel. At the end of the driveway at the back of the Miss Eulalie's house, Jason stood staring at the uprooted live oak tree, one branch pushed through the roof of the guest house. A large hole gaped beneath the leaves. Shingles littered the yard.

As she stared at Jason, the dream image of him in and out of his toga flooded back to Merrill. Heat stained her cheeks. She felt a tingling in her stomach as she remembered every explicit second of her fantasy. She turned off the motor and waited a second, calming herself. She couldn't face him until she had pushed her memories out of her mind.

When she was calm again, Merrill opened the car door and stepped out. Jason gave her a hot look that practically melted the soles of her shoes to the gravel. He looked as though he hadn't slept much. Dark stubble covered his chin, and his long hair was disheveled and sexy. Merrill fought the urge to run her fingers through his hair.

She studied the tree and then Jason. He shrugged at her, and her heart did a little flip flop. A lock of black hair had fallen over his forehead, and he casually pushed it back. His dark eyes sparkled with amusement.

"I don't get it," Jason said, running his hand through his hair. "That tree was on the other side of the garage. It's like it did a somersault right over the roof and landed here."

She looked at the hole in the roof. "Is that your place?"

"It was. The hole is right between the bathroom and the bedroom."

"Where are you going to live now?" Merrill asked, afraid of what his answer might be.

He turned and just looked at the main house, saying nothing.

He couldn't live with her! How would she control herself with him just down the hallway? The force of her dream returned. She remembered every illicit detail. Every place his mouth had kissed and his hand caressed. She was amazed she didn't incinerate on the spot.

His eyes flickered over her. "Are you all right? You look a little flushed." He touched her forehead. "You're hot."

She shrugged him away. "I'm fine. It's the humidity."

"Maybe you should go in the house. You look like you're going to faint."

"I am not some wilted lily. I've lived in Charleston most of my life. I can handle a little humidity."

"Don't jump down my throat. I'm concerned. If you're not healthy, who's going to take care of all the legal work for Psycho?"

"I've never let a client down yet. I don't intend to start now." She stepped back, afraid he'd touch her again, and she'd act out her dream right here on the lawn in glorious living color. "You didn't answer my question."

"Calm down, Scarlett. There are seven empty bedrooms over there." He jerked his thumb at the main house. "I know you won't mind."

She grimaced. "Do I have a choice?" She couldn't have him living in such close proximity. She was too attracted to him. She didn't trust herself. Her grandmother would have a real heart attack, and not the one she'd threatened to have earlier.

"Miss Prescott, a force of nature changed our agreement."

"How long will it take you to fix the roof?"

He grinned. "You make me think you don't want my company."

"It's not your company that worries me." It was her own erotic dreams.

"So what's worrying you?"

Merrill tapped her foot on the ground. "My grandmother lives right around the corner, and she is connected in some way to every gossip in Charleston." She could see the city's old ladies exchanging information over tea and crumpets like they were playing cards. Her reputation would be in shreds.

Jason crossed his arms over his chest. "You're as safe with me as you would be with a big brother."

Hurt, she said, "I didn't mean to imply you were anything but a gentleman." He didn't think she was attractive. How demoralizing. She was having erotic dreams about him, and he wasn't interested in her one iota. She might be safe from him, but was he safe from her? "When can you start on the roof?"

"That could be a while." He peered at the ruined roof. "I can't just slap some plywood on top of the guest house to plug the hole and call it done. I have to order special materials to meet historical standards."

Merrill frowned. "The Blue-haired Bunch strikes again. I see you've had dealings with the Historical Committee yourself. One of my clients battled them for five years and a very nasty law suit to get permits to build a sun porch. Well, Mr. Stavros, if the Committee dictates this, I'm powerless to prevent it."

When she was a kid, with her parents taking her hither and yon in a Volkswagen bus from commune to commune, she had felt powerless. As helpless then as she felt now. Some greater force had taken hold of her life and refused to let go. If she hadn't loved Miss Eulalie so much, she'd be mad at the old woman for dying on her and leaving her in this mess.

"Not to worry," he said, "I've already ordered the materials, and they'll be here in a week or so. Right now, I'm going to patch it."

"Fine." She hooked her thumbs in the belt loops of her jeans. "Let's get this over with. Where do you keep your tools?"

"Are you going to help me?"

"Of course." Not having money had made her very self-sufficient. She couldn't afford to call a carpenter every time a nail popped out of the wall.

"This I've got to see."

A bright-red pickup truck turned into the driveway, a blue tarp covering the back. The truck parked next to her car, and Lula jumped out. A teenage boy opened the passenger door and leaped out with all the energy only a teenager would have.

"Hey, Boss," Lula called. "Where do you want all your stuff?" She flipped back the tarp to reveal Merrill's luggage, computer and file boxes.

"Just find a bedroom with a bed and drop it," Merrill ordered. She didn't care what room she had. As long as it had a bed in it, she could make do.

Jason glanced at the truck. "Lula, isn't it?"

Lula fluttered mascara-drenched eyelashes. "Oh, yes, Mr. Stavros."

Jason blushed. "Miss Prescott's bedroom is on the second floor, all the way to the end of the hall and on the right."

Lula poked him in the chest. "Where's yours, Sugar?"

"Lula!" Merrill cried.

Jason's blush deepened.

Merrill wanted to smack Lula. She delighted much too much in being Southern. She wanted to apologize, but she figured that would only embarrass Jason more. When was Lula going to grow up?

"Is that all you brought with you?" Jason asked.

Merrill shrugged, glad he didn't comment on Lula's come on. "Do I need more? I can certainly go get my bed, but I assumed I'd have one here."

He gave her a strange look.

"Did you expect me to pack every item I owned?"

"Yes," he grinned at her. "I've never known a woman to travel light before."

She laughed. "You've met your first one, Mr. Stavros. I have traveled light from a very young age."

"I thought we were going to drop the Mr. Stavros bit for Jason. I keep wanting to turn around and look for my father."

Formality gave her comfort. Living in such close quarters with him, she needed to keep her distance. Something about Jason Stavros threatened the order she tried so hard to keep around her. She didn't know why she needed such control over her life, but she felt it necessary for her own peace of mind. "Well, Mr. Stavros...Jason. All right."

"That wasn't so hard, was it?" His eyes twinkled at her. "Let me tell Lula we're going to patch the roof, and then we'll get started." He headed toward the garage.

***

Jason held the ladder as she climbed up. She made slow progress, as she carried a toolbox in one hand. He noticed how the well-worn jeans just clung to her tight butt. Women should have butts like that. Merrill's was gently rounded and much too enticing, reminding him of his dream of the night before. He never had dreams like that. Not even of the centerfolds in the nudie magazines he'd hidden under his mattress during his wild high school days.

She reached the roof line, turned around, and looked down at him. "Are you coming?"

"Give me a second here." He had to calm himself down. He didn't think he should be up there swinging a hammer with a hard-on. He'd get distracted and hit himself in the head.

"Fine," she grumbled. "Finish your daydream."

He leaned his heated forehead against the cool metal of the extension ladder. He wasn't going to get through this. Not living in the same house with her, sharing the only working bathroom. Except for the master bath, which had already been updated, the plumbing in the upstairs bathrooms needed replacing, and he'd turned off the water to all of them. And of course, the tree had to land right on his bathroom. He couldn't use the ladies' bathrooms, because with them gone, he'd ripped out the toilets intending to take advantage of their absence. He couldn't share with William, because William's bath was the size of a postage stamp. He was stuck.

He started climbing the ladder, lugging his own toolbox. Merrill moved sideways across the roof like a pro. She wasn't kidding. She had done this before. Now, why would a woman as rich as she was know how to work on a roof? She was too complicated. After his ex-wife, he didn't date complicated women.

She stopped at the hole and, with the claw edge of the hammer, started levering shingles away to reveal the tree limb embedded in the roof. She opened her box, pulled out a saw, and started ripping into the limb. She'd used a saw before. Her strokes were long and even. And each movement of her arms jiggled her breasts beneath the clinging fabric of her white t-shirt. Sweat popped out on his forehead.

Merrill stopped sawing and looked at him. "I can do this myself."

"Okay." He plopped himself down on the crown of the roof to watch her. He liked watching her. She was slender, with nicely toned muscles that he hadn't expected. "So tell me. How did a girl like you learn to use a saw?"

"Knowledge is power, and I've always believed you should know a little something about everything."

"What do you know about baseball?"

"That it's not a sport, and football is the only thing that counts."

Jason could have fallen off the roof. She had just insulted his beloved Yankees.

Down below, Merrill's secretary and the boy with her, had unloaded the truck. Lula waved at Jason and he waved back. Then she disappeared into the house with the last load in her arms.

Jason tried to picture Merrill watching a football game. Football didn't seem like her style. She wasn't the beer and hot dog type. Or was she? At every turn, she surprised him.

But nothing that she did in the real world surprised him as much as what she'd done in his dream last night. She'd been a tiger, a voracious lover who'd left him panting for more. She couldn't be like that in the real world. She was too demure, too ladylike. Her seductive appearance was deceptive. Just like Serena's.

Good. Think of The Bitch. That would snap him out of this dangerous attraction. All he had to do was remember how Serena had conned him and taken him on a roller coaster ride through hell.

***

They worked on the roof patch until they ran out of nails.

As they climbed down the ladder, Jason said, "I'll call the hardware store and have them send over a few more boxes. We'll finish the job later."

"Okay. I'll help you finish then." Merrill stepped into the kitchen, splashed water on her face, then fixed herself a tall glass of ice water and a second for Jason. "Right now, I'm going to check on Lula," Merrill announced when they'd finished their water. She felt a little guilty about leaving Lula to carry all that heavy stuff.

When she entered the living room, Merrill stopped so quickly Jason bumped into her. The room was empty. Not one stick of furniture was anywhere in sight. "What happened to all the furniture?" Miss Eulalie had had pieces dating all the way back to the Renaissance.

"Except what was in her bedroom, and the furniture in one of the guest rooms. She sold most everything at auction and gave the proceeds to charity." Jason replied. "She said I could decorate the house any way I wanted."

A fresh spurt of grief for the grand old lady filled Merrill. Miss Eulalie had known she was dying. For the first time, she realized the dogs were nowhere around. "Where is Psyche's Folly?"

"I locked both dogs in the garage to keep them out of the way. The last time I checked, Buster was teaching Psycho the fine art of being lazy. He's a pro."

Merrill smiled. He really had a nice sense of humor. Much like her father. "You are a very funny man."

"It's a gift."

The front door popped open. Belle Boyd Beaumont entered and, after one look around, screamed. "My God! What have you done with my aunt's furniture?" She turned in a circle. "The Chippendale armoire is gone." She covered her heart with one hand. "And the Regency sofa." She ran into the parlor. "And the Mings. Where are my Mings? I'm goin' to faint." She waved a hand in front of her face. "Tell me you saved the Jefferson secretary."

"Afraid not." Jason shook his head.

Merrill tried not to laugh. "I'm sorry you're distressed, Mrs. Beaumont." Belle Boyd looked ridiculous and had just proved how greedy she truly was.

"Where are the Empire corner chairs?" Belle pulled a lace handkerchief out of her purse and began to cry. "I know my aunt wanted me to have those chairs." She dabbed her eyes. "Where are they?"

Jason tried to hide a smile, but the corners of his mouth lifted upward. He looked at his watch. "Auction block at Christie's. They were probably sold three hours ago."

"In New York City?" She fainted. Her chiffon dress flew up to expose bird-thin legs. Merrill could see Belle struggling with the art of fainting convincingly while attempting to shove her skirt back down over her knees to maintain her decorum.

Jason glanced at Merrill. "Was I supposed to catch her?"

"I'm not sure." Merrill had to admire the other woman.

"Should I leave her?"

Merrill glanced around. "Where would you put her?"

"I could take her to the kitchen and lay her on the counter. Splash a little water in her face."

Merrill couldn't help the small grin that escaped. She knew she should feel sorry for Belle, but couldn't seem to dredge up the emotion. "Okay, let's get her a glass of water."

J. D. Bidwell entered. He saw his sister stretched out on the floor, moaning. He rushed to her side. "Belle!" He glared at Jason. "You did this to her, didn't you?"

Jason shrugged. "She fainted all by herself."

J. D. yanked on one of Belle's arms, pulling her into a sitting position. "Help me get her up."

Merrill spread her hands. "And put her where? There's no furniture."

Belle moaned. J.D. glanced around as though noticing the empty room for the first time. "Where is all the furniture?" He let go of his sister and stood up to stare. She flopped back on the floor.

"Christie's auctioned the furniture off this morning," Jason said. "If you visited more often, you would have noticed everything was gone."

Merrill wondered if J.D. felt the surgical precision of that cut. She doubted it. J.D. wasn't the sharpest knife in the drawer.

"Our lawyer," J.D. said dramatically, "will get every stick of that furniture back."

Merrill's hackles went up. Belle Boyd and J.D. had hired themselves an attorney. This meant war. They were bound and determined to drag their aunt's good name through the mud, just for some cash.

Belle moaned again. Her eyelids fluttered. She opened her eyes and looked around. "They've pillaged my dear Aunt Eulalie's house."

J.D., recalled to his senses, squatted. He glared at Jason. "You have robbed my aunt of her possessions the same way Sherman violated Charleston."

Jason shook his head. "Blow it out your ear, fancy boy."

Merrill turned away, covering her mouth to stop herself from laughing. William Faulkner must be rolling in his grave. To think he died and missed all this heaving emotion. He could have written a sequel to *The Sound and The Fury.*

"J.D.," Merrill said, "Miss Eulalie obviously had no intention of leaving you or Belle any of her furniture. I'm sure you'll find all the papers in order."

Belle cried, "We'll never get any of it back!" She threw out her arms. "J.D., fetch me a cool glass of water. My head is still spinning."

J.D. rushed off to the kitchen. When he returned, he knelt next to his sister. He dipped his fingers daintily in the water and splashed her face.

Merrill shook her head. "Here, let me." She took the glass of water from J.D. and poured it over Belle Boyd's face.

Belle sat up and spluttered like a fish. "How dare you!"

Merrill ordered, "Get up and get out. You have no right to be here."

Outraged, J.D. helped Belle Boyd to her feet. "You're as demented as my aunt," Belle Boyd screeched.

Jason's gaze narrowed. "Are you saying Eulalie Bidwell was Loony Tunes?"

J.D. responded, "Well I wouldn't put it quite in those base terms."

Jason stepped toward the man. J.D. backed up, a spurt of fear crossing his face.

Merrill wanted to close her eyes so she would miss the carnage. This was going to be ugly.

"Eulalie Bidwell had more sense in her left pinky toe than you two will ever have put together." He pointed at J.D. and Belle.

J.D. held up his hands. "There's no need to threaten us."

"I haven't even begun."

Merrill stepped between Jason and J.D. She put one hand on Jason's chest and a little tingle electrified her. For a second she couldn't remember what she'd been about to say. Her brain seemed paralyzed at the feel of his hard muscles. *Don't you dare swoon, Merrill Prescott,* she scolded herself.

"Gentlemen," her voice sounded breathless. She found she couldn't look at Jason. "I think you should each go to your neutral corners, and let's call this round a draw."

Jason took a deep breath and stepped back, his fists clenched. He didn't like Eulalie's sniveling relatives. Between the two of them, he wondered if they could even find a backbone, much less a brain. How dare they come in here and imply that Eulalie was nuts! Jason would fight to the death to preserve her reputation.

Belle said, "Merrill, I think we could find a way to settle this situation amicably."

Merrill glanced at Jason. "How do you suggest we do that?"

Jason glared at Belle Boyd and J.D. "There will be no settlement. Get the hell out of here."

Merrill raised her hand. "Jason, just a moment. Let's hear them out."

"No." Jason stood firm. "I don't want to hear what they have to say, or listen to their demands. The only thing they want is the money."

Merrill touched his arm. "I want to hear their demands."

"No," he whispered.

"Listen," she whispered back, "if I don't know what they want, I won't be able to fight them."

He nodded reluctantly. "Then I'll listen." He stepped back, surprised at the determined strength in Merrill's face.

She turned to Belle Boyd. "All right. I'm listening."

Belle Boyd leaned against her brother, her face smug. J.D. looked superior, as though he'd already won.

J.D. glanced at his sister. "We are willing to allow the servants to keep their inheritance, and are willing to allow a million dollars for the dog's upkeep, but the property and the rest of the estimated seventy-five million dollar estate will be split evenly between us."

"Greedy jerks," Jason muttered.

Merrill elbowed Jason. "I'll have to think about this. That's quite a bit of money."

Belle Boyd stood up straight. "We are blood kin to Miss Eulalie. It's only logical we get the bulk of the estate."

More like blood-suckers, Jason thought. *Leeches.*

Merrill tilted her head and smiled sweetly at Belle Boyd. "You are Bidwells by marriage. I think if Miss Eulalie wanted you to have the money, she would have made a larger provision for you in her will."

J.D. gave her an oily smile. "I'm sure she would have if she had been of sound mind." He eyed Jason and clicked his tongue.

Merrill colored.

Jason's fury returned. "Spit it out. What are you saying?"

J.D. shrugged. "Think whatever you want."

Merrill clenched her fists. "Are you accusing Jason and me of influencing Miss Eulalie? Don't you think we would have made sure the money was left to us and not the dog, if that were the case?"

Belle Boyd shrugged her shoulders. "Miss Prescott, I think you're a very smart woman. The whole situation looks a little too cozy. Who knows what you two will be up to with all that money?"

"Enough!" Jason grabbed J.D. by the lapels, levered him out the door, across the veranda, and down the stairs to the sidewalk. "You've insulted Eulalie, Merrill, and me. If you so much as look at the front yard, I'll consider it trespassing, and your butt is mine." He let go, and the other man stumbled back.

Belle Boyd rushed down the stairs. "You are such a brute. Such an animal. Are you all right, J.D.?"

Jason took a step toward them, and J.D. backed off the sidewalk onto the grass, his feet sinking into a soft bit of mud. He stared down at his feet. "We'll see you in court, Yankee Man." He stalked away, leaving Belle to trail along behind.

Jason walked back into the empty living room. He brushed his hands off. "I felt good about that. What about you?"

Merrill grinned at him. Lula, standing at the top of the grand staircase, clapped. "Bravo, Mr. Stavros. Bravo." And she dimpled at him with a saucy tilt of her head.

"Stop that, Lula." She turned to Jason. "As an officer of the court, I cannot condone any acts of violence, so I'll have to pretend I didn't see that." But she winked at him.

Lula leaned over the bannister. "Merrill, you need to come up here and see this."

Jason watched Merrill climb the stairs. Her small, heart-shaped butt swung from side to side with a grace that would have made the sun fall out of the sky. He couldn't believe he'd gotten all worked up over her. Yeah, she was beautiful, smart and very classy. He had to stop thinking about her. Under all that class, she had to be just like Serena. Rich women were all the same.

***

Cupid entered Venus' bedroom. Venus reclined, as only Venus could recline, on a huge four-poster bed with velvet hangings, a card table at her side. Mrs. Eulalie Bidwell sat on the other side, smoking a cigar and shuffling the deck of cards.

"Nice going with the tree placement, Ma. It landed perfectly on the roof," Cupid said. "The chainsaw will never be the same."

"Thank you, dear. I hope you'll be able to repair it." Venus languidly waved her hand at Eulalie. "Look who's stopped for a visit."

"Still having a problem with power tools, aren't you dear." Miss Eulalie puffed on her cigar. Eulalie Bidwell looked like a little elf. She had a short, round body and frizzy brown hair surrounding a friendly face.

"Just a little one." Venus held up her hand. "At least I didn't chip a nail. What are we playing?"

"Five card stud, dear." Eulalie shuffled the cards one more time.

"Stud. One of my favorite words."

"Venus," Miss Eulalie stated, "you are so trashy. I love it."

Cupid stared, open-mouthed. Why wasn't Eulalie on her way to the Elysian Fields? Cupid kissed Eulalie on the cheek. "You're as beautiful as ever."

Eulalie smiled demurely. "You say that to all the girls."

"But I always mean it with you."

With a youthful giggle, Eulalie said, "You're so sweet."

A thought occurred to him. "Wait a minute. What are you two plotting?"

Eulalie and Venus grinned. "Nothing," they replied in unison.

"That sounds like something to me. I don't believe you."

Eulalie smiled sweetly at him. "We're just having some girl talk."

Venus fanned her face with her cards. "Don't you trust me?"

"No." Cupid glanced at her cards. She had five aces.

Eulalie set her cards face down on the table. "Your Mama and I have been planning something on the sly for a while now. Venus here told me what she did to alter the will to get Merrill and Jason together. I confess, it never occurred to me to do a joint custody for my dog." She patted Venus' hand. "You are such a clever girl. And you managed to copy my handwriting perfectly."

"How do you think I got custody of Cupid in the divorce from Mars?" Venus said. "He was so busy with the battle of Hastings, he never looked at the paperwork. Besides, a little fraud doesn't hurt anyone, especially if it brings the ideal lovers together. I know Merrill and Jason would be so perfect together."

Cupid took Venus' cards away. "We're out of the mortal business."

Venus snapped her fingers, and the table and cards disappeared.

Eulalie sipped her wine. "Busted," she said merrily. "Venus, I have to get on my way. You know how it is on the Fields—if you don't show up, Pluto gives your condo away." She finished her wine and stood. "I'll leave you to explain to Cupid what's going on."

Venus languidly waved her hand. "Bye, y'all. Come back real soon now, ya hear."

Miss Eulalie disappeared in a puff of smoke.

Cupid rounded on his mother. "What are you doing?"

She looked at her limp hand. "Ah'm practicin' on Plan A, Sugah."

Cupid frowned. He didn't get it. "Practicing?"

"Being a Steel Magnolia. Eulalie suggested it."

"Heavy metal flowers!" Cupid was confused. But his mother did tend to do that to him.

Venus shook her head emphatically. "Don't be so dense, honey-chile. We're goin' undercover, and I'm working on my camouflage."

"I thought we were out of the mortal love business. Jupiter made his new policy retroactive."

She smiled sweetly at him. "Actually, Eulalie and I haven't figured out the whole plan yet, but what Daddy Dahlin' doesn't know isn't going to hurt him. I know what I'm doin.' My love whammy is not subject to 'policy.'"

"A love whammy?" Cupid stared at her. Maybe he should have her committed. Are there insane asylums for gods? Eulalie should be ashamed of herself for encouraging his mother.

Venus snapped her fingers. "Yankee Boy, get with the lingo. You worry too much."

"That is exactly the *laissez faire* attitude that put me on probation in the first place. I can't break any more rules, Ma, not even for you, or I'll be on probation from now until the universe collapses."

"Don't worry, honey-chile, I spoke to Apollo and took care of your little problem."

Suspiciously, he asked, "What did you do?" Her help was what had put him on probation in the first place.

She waved her hand languidly. "I called in a favor. That's all you need to know, dahlin'."

Cupid found his mother to be the most frustrating goddess in the universe. "Mom, whatever you are thinking, you need to stop it now."

Venus sighed. "Don't get your toga in a bunch. I know you're just dying to help me. Your lips may say no, but I know what's in your heart. You have always been a matchmaker, and you will always be a matchmaker. I don't care what some silly old windbag god tells us. If we can't do the job we were born to do, then we may as well just sit around and grow fruit and herd animals the rest of our lives. You know how I hate the outdoors. I figure if I can't get Jason and Merrill together in a first-hand sort of way, I'll do it in a roundabout sort of way."

Cupid decided she'd definitely lost her mind. Venus was a manipulator, a conniver, and a sexpot, but she wasn't a rebel. When faced with rebellion, she pretended it never happened. To think she was defying her father made his eyes twitch. Because whatever punishment she received, he'd be sharing it with her.

But as much as he hated to admit it, she was right. He was the God of Desire. Making people fall in love was his job.

Cupid, don't be a rule-breaker. Just follow Grandpa's orders, and you'll be happier. "I can't help you, Mom."

"Yes, you can, Cupie. You have to help me. You're the only one who can help me." She gave him a sad, pathetic, puppy-dog look.

"Ma, I'm not risking eternity with the Titans. Apollo already has it in for me."

Venus patted his hand. "Don't worry, sweetie. I appealed to my big brother's sense of compassion." She fluttered her eyelashes.

He leaned closer to his mother. "You're blackmailing Apollo, aren't you?"

Venus clutched her chest in a classic dramatic gesture. "Blackmail is such an ugly word." She smiled at him. "I prefer the term—extortion. It is so much more genteel."

"I hate myself for asking, but what are you planning to do about Merrill and Jason?"

Venus lifted her hand and showed him two rings. "Vulcan gave me these."

"Rings?" He eyed the gold circlets in her hand.

"Right. Vulcie says as long as we wear these rings," she handed him the duplicate, "we will be invisible to every god and goddess while we're on Earth in our mortal disguise. Daddy uses these when he wants to step out on Juno." Venus twisted her ring. "He thinks his ring is the only one in existence. But I had Vulcan whip me up a couple spares."

Cupid took the ring and slipped it on his finger. The ring sized itself to fit his chubby hand. "I can't believe Vulcan gave these to you."

Venus elbowed him. "Listen, sonny, let me share a little secret with you. A male has not been invented who can turn me down when I'm wearing nothing but a pair of pink cowgirl boots and a smile."

Cupid stared at his mother. "Yee ha."

She curtsied.

"What do you intend to do with these rings?"

"I don't know yet, but I'm thinking."

He shuddered. His mother's thinking had gotten him into too much trouble in the past. "I'll end up being a dog."

"Well, that's Plan B, Cupid, my boy. That's Plan B."

If I were smart, Cupid thought, *I'd find a nebula and hide for the next hundred years.* He knew, deep in his heart, she would talk him into this, and he didn't want to be talked into it. Because his instincts told him this could only end in disaster. Disaster with his name written all over it.

Four

Merrill stood in the doorway, shocked. The bedroom took her breath away. Her whole apartment in Boston would have fit into the room and there would still be plenty of space left over.

Never in her life had she had such a beautiful bedroom. An Elizabethan four-poster bed with velvet hangings dominated the room. In the corner a marble fireplace gave a sense of decadence. Beside the bank of windows flanking the double doors which opened to the balcony was an Empire sofa. It was flanked by matching chairs upholstered in red satin. A door opened to the bathroom where she could see a claw foot tub, double pedestal sinks and a stained glass window which seemed unusually dark. After a moment, she realized the window was boarded up.

Jason followed her as she walked into the bathroom and stared at the window. She could just make out the outline of The Three Graces, Cupid and Venus flanked by wisteria vines and tiny hummingbirds. "My word. It's beautiful."

Jason nodded in agreement. "Mr. Bidwell commissioned it as a wedding present for Eulalie. It's the first thing I board up when a storm is coming. I'll take the boards down right away. The colors are at their most brilliant when the sun sets."

Merrill stepped back into the bedroom with its extra-large Elizabethan bed. The rich velvet hangings in bright blue gave her a sense of grandeur. The Virgin Queen herself probably didn't have anything so lovely. She felt a moment's dizziness and closed her eyes. When she opened them, she had a mental picture of Jason reclining on the bed with the sheet riding dangerously low on his stomach.

Flustered, she said, "Don't you have something a little less elegant?" She would be lost in that bed. It needed two people.

Jason chuckled. "Only if you don't mind sleeping on the floor with the dogs."

She did mind. "Why would Miss Eulalie sell everything but the furniture in this room? It's worth a fortune."

Jason shrugged. "She liked her comfort and said her bedroom was sexy."

Sexy was the word for it. "Miss Eulalie used the 'S' word?"

"Have you always been a prude?"

She stammered. "I like sex just fine, thank you."

"I'll bet you do," he purred.

She blushed, the erotic dream of the night before coming back to haunt her all over again. How could she get the dream out of her head? Every movement he made brought back certain images. Images that would have made Eulalie blush.

"Don't worry about it. Just go with the flow. Eulalie knew what she was doing."

"But I don't."

He put a finger under her chin and lifted it slightly. "Do you need to have a rational explanation for everything?"

His touch sent shivers of desire spiraling through her body. He moved closer, and she waited for him to kiss her. She wanted the kiss. She could feel his body heat radiating outward, wrapping her in a cloud of sensuality.

Lula waltzed into the room. "Where do you want me to set up your computer?" She giggled and backed out. "Excuse me."

Merrill snapped back to her sensible self and pulled away, embarrassed that she had been caught in a compromising position.

A car horn sounded in the driveway. The door slammed and a voice trilled, "Hi, y'all. We're here."

Merrill stepped onto the balcony and saw a white mini-van with the legend, Marco Mercer: Prince of Chintz on the side. A tall, slender man stood in the driveway. He wore a black turtleneck sweater and matching black pants. His dark hair framed a slender face, pale from little time in the sun.

"Who is that?" Merrill asked as Jason joined her at the wrought iron railing.

"I have no idea who he is. Did you call a decorator?"

Merrill glared at him. "Why would I call anybody? I didn't know I was going to have to live here."

A slender woman of incredible beauty stepped out of the van and followed the man to the house.

The doorbell rang, and Merrill and Jason ran down the stairs to answer it.

"Hello," the young man lisped, "I'm Marco Mercer. And you must be the happy couple. Miss Eulalie told me all about the two of you. Congratulations."

Jason frowned. "Congratulations for what?"

"Silly boy," the woman purred, "your nuptials of course. Let me be the first to kiss the groom."

The woman grabbed Jason by the shirt, her lips pursed. Merrill put her hand on the woman's shoulder and gently tugged her back. "I don't think so."

The assistant smiled. "I'm sorry. Forgive my boldness, I get carried away by true love."

"I think you're mistaken," Jason said. "We're not married."

The young man said, "But Miss Eulalie said—."

Jason interrupted. "You must have misunderstood her."

"That's always a possibility." He pressed a business card into Jason's hand. "Miss Eulalie spoke to me briefly, telling me that she'd sold all her furniture and suggested I and my assistant pop in and help you."

The young man stood in the center of the empty living room and unrolled a tape measure. He stood with one hand under his chin and the other on his hip as he surveyed the fireplace. "Beautiful," he lisped. "Absolutely beautiful." Buster and Psyche sniffed at him and sat down, their heads tilted as they stared up at him. "Doggy dahling," the man said to Psyche. "Don't you think this is beautiful? Miss Eulalie couldn't have given us a better description."

Psyche wagged her tail. Buster barked.

Jason drew Merrill to the side. "What's that 'get up' the guy is wearing. This is June. No one wears black in June."

"He's one of 'those' kind."

"What kind is that?"

"The Bohemian kind. You know, an *artiste*."

Marco walked around the room, clapping his hands. "I'm having a creative orgasm." Buster followed him. Marco patted Buster on the head.

The woman gave him an adoring look. "Of course, you are." She ruffled Psyche's ears.

Jason whispered to Merrill, "I've never seen the dog take to strangers like this."

She felt the heat of his breath on her ear, and her knees nearly buckled. He could have been talking about plaster, and Merrill would have gotten excited. His breath tickled her skin, and she smothered a giggle.

Jason cleared his throat. "Excuse me, Mr. Mercer, I don't know what you're doing here."

Marco and the woman started to titter as though they shared some inside joke. "Miss Eulalie told us to come."

"But Miss Eulalie's dead."

Marco Mercer and the woman exchanged looks. "We know that."

Merrill stared at them. "Pardon me?"

Jason ran his hands through his hair. "Until we get this all straightened out, I don't think you should be here."

The woman tilted one shoulder at him flirtatiously. "You are so masterful. I can see why the North lost the war."

Jason looked confused. "Don't you mean the South?"

"Silly, silly me." She giggled. "Of course, I mean the South. You got me all flustered." She waved a hand in front of her face. "Here." She handed Jason a piece of paper.

Merrill stared. Where had the paper come from? It hadn't been in the woman's hand a moment ago.

Jason said, "Who are you?" He stared at the paper.

"Oh gracious, where are my manners?" She covered her heart with one hand. "I'm Violet. Violet Summers. Mr. Mercer's special assistant." She held out her hand to Jason's lips.

He stared at Violet's fingers. Then he carefully shook her hand while Merrill bit her lip to keep her laughter under control.

"What is this?" Jason asked.

"It's a contract." Violet fluttered the paper. "Miss Eulalie retained us to help you redecorate the house."

Marco closed his eyes and rested the back of his hand against his forehead. "I'm seeing a sofa. A huge sofa. Miss Eulalie did suggest a bone-shaped sofa."

"Don't you mean bone-colored?" Merrill took the contract to examine it. The signature looked all right, but she wanted a closer look.

"Of course. What was I thinking? Though I really did like the dog house with air-conditioning, designed like Tara. You know, that anti-bell-um house from the movie. What do you think, doggy?" Buster sat down, his eyes rapt with adoration for the man.

"I just don't think this is an appropriate time," Merrill said.

Marco put his hands on his hips. "Well if that doesn't put the brakes on my creative Muse."

Merrill shook her head. She felt as though she'd stepped into another dimension. Usually she was a 'live and let live' type of person, but these two were weird and would take a lot of getting used to.

"Mr. Stavros," Merrill tilted her head toward the kitchen. "May I speak to you in private?"

Violet made little shooing motions with her hands. "You two go off and be alone. Fall in love now, while you're in there. Never mind us. We're just going to decorate."

Merrill grabbed Jason's hand and jerked him into the kitchen. "Did you know about these people?"

He looked as bewildered as she felt. He tapped his head. "No, but Elvis has left the building."

"Elvis never showed up," Merrill retorted. "Tell me something. How did Miss Eulalie settle on these decorators?"

"I don't have a clue."

She studied the contract. It seemed legitimate.

Jason patted her arm. "They seem harmless."

"I've had experience with con men before. Harmless is their stock and trade. There has to be a loophole with these designers. They are way too cornball."

Jason leaned his hip against the corner of the counter. "You think Eulalie was crazy, don't you?"

"I don't think anything of the kind. But I can't believe she'd hire these two buffoons. And if Belle Boyd and J.D. get hold of them, that money is already in their bank accounts. And you're not helping matters any."

Jason frowned. "I'm the only one defending her. Who cares if Eulalie wanted to paper her walls with that money? It belonged to her, and she could do whatever she damn well pleased with it."

A sharp suspicion rose in her. Merrill remembered how much money, to the penny, Miss Eulalie had spent on the restoration she'd hired Jason to do. Maybe she should get a forensic accountant in to scrutinize the expenses. If Miss Eulalie could be taken in by Violet Summers and the Chintz King, then Jason Stavros wouldn't have broken a sweat swindling her out of her money. As far as Merrill was concerned, she would have every paper clip, every nail accounted for.

"You don't trust me, do you?" Jason suddenly asked, as if reading her mind.

"I don't know what to think right now." She was not ready to lay all her cards on the table. "But I do know that Belle Boyd and J.D. could crucify us if their lawyer gets a whiff of these two imbeciles. Miss Eulalie appointed us custodians of the dog and executers of her will, and we are obligated to see that her last wishes are carried out as she specified. I don't care if I have to fight Belle, J.D. and any lawyer they hire to end of the earth. I will even take you to the mat, Stavros. It doesn't matter what my personal opinion of Miss Eulalie's financial decision is. There's nothing I won't do to protect her good name. Do you understand me? So you just make certain your house is in order."

Jason crossed his arms over his chest, frowning. "Are you through?"

She could only nod, not trusting her voice. She'd said a lot more than she should have.

"I know exactly what type of person you are," Jason continued.

Merrill took a deep breath. "What type of person am I?" She knew she wasn't going to like the answer.

"You play at being a lawyer because it fills the void in your over-privileged life."

Merrill snapped, "You make it sound like money bought my degree."

A shadow crossed his face. He seemed to grow distant, even though he was only a few feet away from her. "You think because you were born with a silver spoon in your mouth you are entitled to more than you deserve."

"What do you know about my life?"

"I know women like you, Merrill Prescott the Fourth. You grew up thinking you could judge a person by the fork he uses, or the way he speaks, or what he does for a living."

"You're wrong," she replied.

"I'm not wrong."

Merrill felt a strange grief fill her. Money had gotten her nothing. Other than a few years of privilege as a child, everything had been gone by the time she was five. Her uncle had gambled on a pyramid scheme and lost almost everything. Nana had been living on her dreams of the past and the interest from a trust fund her son had been unable to break into.

"You blue blood money types," Jason went on, "are all alike, whether you're from New York, San Francisco or Charleston. Every once in a while you go beyond the barriers of your safe little world to get a taste of real life, but it never lasts long. You tire of your toys easily."

"Is that how you thought of Miss Eulalie?" His contempt wounded her. He had no idea what he was talking about, and she wondered why she felt the need to impress on him that she wasn't the way he said.

He laughed. "Eulalie was real. She was funny, kind and smart. And, by the way, she was sane." His face took on a fierce demeanor. "Saner than you and me put together."

Merrill stopped herself from being too impressed by his impassioned declaration. Jason Stavros was good looking enough to make a woman forget. But when he opened his mouth and started speaking those passionate words about Miss Eulalie and blue-blood, he almost had Merrill convinced.

She'd already come up against some of the best lawyers in the South. She knew good rhetoric when she heard it. This man was good. He could be a lawyer himself. He had that strong sense of sincerity any lawyer needed to convince a jury that he was right and the opposition wrong. It was a trait lawyers shared with good con men.

She took another look at the contract and then waved it in front of Jason.

"What?" he asked.

"I found the loophole."

***

Venus and Cupid stood in the middle of Miss Eulalie's empty living room. Venus held out a compact mirror. Merrill and Jason were reflected on the shiny surface.

"Do you think I'm dumb?" Venus asked.

"No," Cupid said. "We're just playing a part. Don't worry, Ma. You're smart like a fox." He zapped the wall, and a layer of yellow wallpaper appeared on the surface.

"I know I'm beautiful. I just don't want people to think I'm stupid." Venus pointed a finger, and the yellow was replaced by blue paper. "I hate yellow. I don't want people to think I'm stupid."

Cupid patted her on the arm. "No way." He snapped his fingers, and a zig zag pattern in blue and green appeared.

Venus grimaced at the wall. "I don't understand how we're going to get these two together." She snapped her fingers. The blue and green dripped away, revealing a pink and purple marbleized pattern.

"That's hideous, Ma." A spark of electricity danced down his arm. The pink and purple became white with black stripes. "That's because we're not supposed to get them together anymore." He pointed at the ceiling. "Remember 'the edict' from on high?"

Buster whined and leaned against Cupid's leg. "Thank you for reminding me, Buster." He looked at his mother. "They have to go outside, Ma. You know. Excuse me a minute." Cupid opened the front door for the two dogs, and they jumped down the steps to sniff at the bushes.

Venus stamped her foot. "I'm the love goddess. No one can take away my abilities." She snapped her fingers. The glass in one of the front windows cracked. Venus jumped and looked around.

Cupid pointed at the window, and the glass repaired itself. "Mom, that was a close one. Will you be careful?" When he snapped his fingers this time the wall color turned to black.

"Sorry. I just don't understand what Daddy is up to."

"Now, Mom, I know Gramps. Most of the time, he's a manipulative, lying, self-centered, egotistical, power-hungry kind of guy, but he has his heart in the right place. He does care for these mortals. And maybe he's right. Maybe they should start muddling their own way through their lives. What have we done as gods?

Take, for instance, Mars. All those wars. And what did they accomplish?"

"But..." Venus interrupted, "...that's his job." She flicked her hand at the wall, and huge green vines with gigantic orange flowers twined their way up it.

Cupid replaced the vines with tulips. "What about Juventas and her cult of youth? People are afraid of growing old, of getting slower, of sagging here and there."

Venus drew back. "Don't talk about growing old! You're scaring me, Cupie." The tulips became fuschia orchids.

"See. That's exactly what I mean. Maybe we should just let them work things out for themselves." He crooked his finger, and lilies appeared on the wall.

Venus tilted her head, her hands planted on her hips. "If we let that happen, what are we going to do with our days? I don't see too many of us developing hobbies. What am I supposed to do, take up rock-climbing?" She spread her hands out in front of her. "I'll chip my nails. I was promised a life-long career as the Goddess of Love."

Cupid shook his head. "Jupiter overthrew the Titans because they over-stayed their welcome."

"Son," Venus interrupted, shaking a finger at him. "Who's been teaching you your history? Jupiter wanted their job, and that had nothing to do with over-staying their welcome. Do you know what your grandfather used to do before he 'elevated' himself? He was the God of Small Rodents: rats, weasels and shrews."

"Are weasels rodents?"

Venus threw up her hands. "Does it matter? He was ambitious."

Cupid studied the lilies. They needed more color. Blood red paint seeped across the flowers. "Can we get back to the matter at hand? Jason doesn't trust Merrill. Merrill doesn't trust Jason. This isn't going to be a walk in the park."

"Hm!" Venus touched her chin. "Then we have to do something."

"Like what, considering the new restriction?"

Suddenly, Venus cupped her ear. "Hush. Psyche is trying to tell me something."

Psyche's Folly and Buster were barking up a storm. Cupid heard movement in the hallway, and in the next moment, Jason rushed into the living room. Quickly Cupid snapped his fingers, and the walls returned to their normal ivory color before Jason noticed.

***

Jupiter stood in front of the mirror, singing. He snapped his fingers. A crisp white suit appeared on his body, and a black string bow-tie tied itself around his neck. He stepped back to admire himself. "I do declare, I look like a fine Southern dandy." He grinned at himself. "Rhett Butler has nothing on you, Jupie Boy." He liked the way he looked—like the old guy who dug chicken. As flamboyant as the Colonel was, Jupiter couldn't present himself this way. He had to look young, virile, handsome and sophisticated. What would snare Merrill Prescott? "Elegance, refinement and an educated manner."

"Are you talking to yourself again?" Juno asked as she stepped into his bedroom. She stopped and stared at him. "What are you up to?"

"Nothing," he answered just a little too quickly.

"You don't look like *nothing*." She stepped back to study him. "You look like...." She glared at him, suspiciously.

"Now dear," Jupiter cautioned. "What did Siggy say about trust?"

Her brow cleared and she smiled at him. "Are you getting all dressed up for me?"

"Sort of. I thought I'd take a little trip down Memory Lane."

"Going to visit one of your old girlfriends?"

"Junie." He wrapped his arms around her. "Sweetie. Honey. Love muffin."

She twisted around to glare at him. "Don't you 'love muffin' me. We need to talk."

"About what?"

"Do you still want to go to that couple's retreat on Mount Olympus? I think some of the Greek gods are going to be there."

Jupiter tried to think. If he agreed to go, maybe she'd take off and let him pursue his current interest. But then he'd be stuck going. The last thing he wanted was to spend the next twenty years talking about his so-called passive-aggressive tendencies.

"Jupie, I have to speak to you about something."

"About what?"

She patted his arm tentatively. "The gods and goddesses are complaining about your new policy."

"They're not complaining to me."

"You'd zap them into the next universe if they did, so they came to me."

"Why does everyone make me out to be such an ogre?"

"Must I explain, Jupie?"

He waved his hand. The floor opened up, and Fortuna stood in front of the craps table in Las Vegas with a huge stack of chips in front of her. "Look at that. Fortuna is having the time of her life." He waved again, and a second picture appeared. "Look at the Fates. Nona, Decuma and Morta are making a quilt instead of spinning the thread of human destiny. See how happy they are. And Ceres is running stark naked through a field of barley, filled with such cheerfulness." He caressed his wife's cheek. "We haven't had a decent vacation since the beginning of time. Let's take some time off. Visit the South Pole. You always did like sitting with the penguins."

Juno crossed her arms over her ample chest. She tapped her fingers against her arm. "Vacation, huh? When do you want to go?"

He'd distracted her. Jupiter had to think fast. "The trend is for separate vacations. You go your way, and I'll go mine."

"When you're going your way, will you be going alone?"

"Junie! My days of infidelity are long over. I was thinking of getting together with a couple of the boys. You know, Bacchus, Pluto, Janus and I have been talking about going out into the woods and being one with the forest."

Juno tilted her head at him. "You mean you want to pick berries, and not bathe or shave." Her distaste showed on her face.

"We're reaffirming our connection to our primitive selves, so we can come home and be better husbands and life partners."

Her foot tapped furiously. "Have you been watching infomercials again? I told you, Jupie, those messages are bull."

Jupiter kissed his wife on the tip of her nose. "Maybe, but I think this would be a good time to get to know my inner child. I think you need to do the same thing with some of the girls. Call up Diana, or get Minerva out of her books. Go see your mother. She has a nice place on Fiji."

The suspicious look did not leave her eyes. "I'll think about it. But under one condition, dear husband."

"And that is, dear?" He gave her his best disarming smile.

"When we return from our vacation. We're going to have a talk about your new policy. And if it hasn't worked, then I expect you to put things back the way they were."

"Of course. Juno, you've always been a fierce negotiator." He smiled inwardly. By the time Juno returned from her vacation, he'd have sampled the fair Merrill many times over and be ready to move on to lusher fields. Juno would never suspect a thing.

"All right, Jupiter. You have a deal." She snapped her fingers and disappeared.

"Enjoy yourself." *I will*, he thought. He reached into his jewelry box for his mystic ring. He kissed the gold and slipped it on his finger. Seconds later, he walked up the steps to Blythe Prescott's mansion, ready to present himself as a possible suitor for Merrill's hand. He transformed into the epitome of genteel Southern manhood.

Merrill Prescott, watch out!

Five

Jason opened the front door, ready to tackle the dogs. They weren't vicious or overly protective of the property, but they could be nuisances to visitors. "Psyche. Buster. In the house. Now."

The dogs obediently turned and trotted back inside, heading toward the kitchen. They stopped once to sniff at Violet's shoes, but Violet waved them away.

Jason studied their visitors. An elegant, older woman hung on the arm of a young man dressed in a gray suit. The man looked like a greyhound with a white straw hat shading his brow. He held a bouquet of flowers in one hand, while the woman had tucked her fingers around the other.

The shape of the woman's face and eyes were the same as Merrill's. This had to be the grandmother. For a second, he saw Merrill as she would look in sixty years. The grandmother had a rare beauty that transcended time. Despite the advancement of age, her eyes were youthful and her mouth quirked in a captivating smile that was the exact duplicate of Merrill's smile. She wore youthful clothes that looked perfect on her. No sensible, lace-up granny shoes or shapeless dresses. This woman was elegant and regal. Her white hair was braided and wrapped around her head like a crown. She wore a navy blue dress with a matching jacket that fit her slender body to perfection. Her dark blue eyes gave him the once-over with such sharpness he thought she'd bored into his soul and seen all his secrets.

She shook her cane at him. "Young man, where is my granddaughter?"

"You must mean Merrill." Jason stood aside to allow the woman and her companion into the house.

"And whom did you think I meant, young man?" She rapped her silver-headed cane on the floor. Before he could answer, she stopped in the center of the living room, frowning. "What happened to all the furniture? Have Eulalie's low-down relatives taken everything already? She's not even cold in her grave." She tapped the man on the arm. "Carter, see what happens when you can't control the greedy people in the family?"

The man nodded solemnly. "I know all about controlling members of my family."

The man held out his hand to Jason. "I'm Carter Rutledge-Shelby."

Jason shook the man's hand. His grip was light and his flesh soft. Mr. Rutledge-Shelby hadn't done a lick of hard labor in his whole life. And his name. Didn't anybody have just plain old names around here? What was wrong with Jimmy or Bobby or Vinnie? They were good street names. Carter sounded like he should be sitting on the veranda, drinking mint juleps and speculating on the price of cotton.

A clatter sounded from the window. Jason, Carter and Merrill's grandmother all turned to stare at Violet. The footstool had fallen over, and Violet stood to one side, one hand over her heart, the other wound tight with filmy fabric.

"Mr. Mercer," she said in a breathless little voice, "may I speak to you in private?" She glanced at Jason. "Sorry. Decoratin' emergency." With a big, toothy smile, she pulled Mercer out of the room, her heels clicking on the floor in rapid succession.

Jason gladly watched them leave. At least they wouldn't have to deal with them again. Damn con artists. Thinking they could profit from Eulalie's death. As soon as he got rid of Granny and the dandy, he'd get rid of the pseudo-decorators.

Blythe Prescott stared after Violet and Marco as they beat a retreat. "Who are they?"

"Decorators."

"What are you doing with decorators? Eulalie is dead. And where are all Eulalie's things? This was a perfectly good house just as it was."

Jason replied, "The decorators are just temporary. And Eulalie put all her furniture up for auction."

"Auction?" Blythe Prescott looked horrified. "All those priceless antiques. How could she get rid of her heritage like that? Like it was nothing but used Kleenex. Some of her pieces have been in her family since before the Revolution."

Jason had understood Eulalie's decision, especially after meeting J.D. and Belle Boyd. Once Eulalie explained everything was going to charity, he found he'd admired and respected her even more.

Rutledge-Shelby put an arm around Mrs. Prescott. "Now Miss Blythe, you calm yourself down. Some people have no respect for the past." He glanced at Jason imperiously. "Do you think you could find the time to offer the lady a glass of water or lemonade, or did Miss Eulalie sell all the glassware, too?"

Jason didn't know whether to be offended or not. He was hardly a servant, but good manners did suggest a polite response. "Sure. No problem." Even he could fill a glass from the tap. "While I'm getting water, I'll search down Merrill."

He left, knowing he should have offered Merrill's grandmother a chair, or directed her to one. He hurried to the kitchen. Violet and Marco stood in the hallway. Their whispered conversation held an odd urgency, and Jason figured they were plotting on how to bilk the estate.

Violet spied him and riffled her fingers at him. "Hi, there. We're just hashing out some details. Nothing to worry about. Everythin's fine. Everythin's peachy."

For con artists, they were the oddest people Jason had ever known. He shook his head as he moved down the hallway toward the kitchen. He was in a madhouse.

***

Venus slammed one hand into the palm of the other. "I knew it! I knew this 'new policy' was a scam."

"Calm down. What are you talking about?" Cupid patted her arm. "Remember the Northridge quake. Breathe in. Breathe out. Now a deep cleansing breath."

Venus' lips narrowed. "He's going to ruin it for me. I know he is."

"Who?" Cupid was growing more puzzled by the moment.

"That low down, mangy, flea-bitten hound dog."

"You're taking this Southern *schtick* too far. What dog? Jason's dog?"

"Your grandfather," she hissed. "That's who."

Cupid frowned. "What does Jupiter have to do with this?"

She stared at him. "Cupid, have you been sipping the ambrosia again? Didn't you see Carter what's-his-name?"

Cupid shrugged. "Yeah. So what?"

"It's *Daddy Dearest* in disguise."

Cupid's mouth fell open. "Carter Rutledge-Shelby is Gramps!"

"He's wearing his mystic ring!"

"Do you think he recognized us?" Cupid glanced worriedly at the doorway.

Venus held up her hand and twirled her own mystic ring. "He never even noticed us. He was too busy being Mr. Down Home Southern Gentleman. I need to find out what he's up to."

Cupid looked out the door. "Wait a minute. If you go in there, guns blazing, he's going to know we're violating his policy."

"He's violating it himself." Venus paced back and forth, agitated.

Cupid had never seen her so angry. "But, he's the boss god. With a blink of his eye, he could send us... I don't even want to think about where he can send us. Someplace where I would have to wear polyester for the rest of my life."

Venus stamped her foot. "I don't care. He's moving in on my territory. I do the love matches around here."

Cupid didn't relish going up against his grandfather. "But don't you have to find out what he's doing first?"

"I already know he's up to no good."

Cupid looked down at the mystic ring on his finger. "But, if you talk to him, he'll see your ring. He won't know who you are, but he'll know you're a god. And he's not going to have to overwork any gray cells to figure out it's you and your trusty sidekick, me. You're the only one with the guts to pull off something this devious."

"True." Venus paused in her pacing. "I hate it when you're logical."

She obviously hadn't thought things through yet. Cupid shrugged. "It's a gift."

"What to do? What to do?" She twisted the ring on her finger.

"The first thing we have to do is figure out why he's here. And we have to do it without being seen."

"All right. Let me think on this, and I'll come up with a plan."

Cupid groaned. His mother and thinking. What a disastrous combination!

***

Merrill waited on the phone. One of her police contacts was running a computer check on the supposed decorators. Psyche's Folly lay at her feet, her head resting on her dainty paws. For some reason the dog had taken a liking to her, and Merrill didn't know how she felt about it. Her parents' lifestyle had not been conducive to pets, and Nana absolutely refused to deal with animals.

She reached down and patted the dog's head. The animal looked up at her, her dark brown eyes filled with adoration.

Jason entered the kitchen, his face drawn into troubled lines. The sunlight bounced off his black hair, adding a blue sheen. He had an air of earthy sexuality that both attracted her and unnerved her. He seemed so at ease with himself, like he had nothing to prove. His confidence showed in the self-assured way he walked, the way he held his head, and the directness of his gaze. Merrill had never felt as confident as that.

She had been awkward and gangly as a child. Confidence had never been her strong suit, even after Harvard. No matter how she tried, she never seemed to get over being a wallflower. Over the years, she'd learned to put on a good facade, and sometimes she even felt brave, but then someone like Jason Stavros came along and rocked her sense of hard-won security. "What's wrong?"

"Your grandmother is here with some guy named Carter Rutledge-Shelby."

Just from the way he said 'Carter Rutledge-Shelby', she knew he loathed the man.

"Just what I need," she sighed as she as cradled the phone against her ear. "Nana with another one."

"Another one what?"

"Husband material. She will not rest until I am safely shackled to a proper Southern gentleman."

He grinned. "Not your style, huh?"

Jason Stavros was beginning to look like her style. "Nana believes I only need three things to be happy—a wealthy husband, a Southern address, and lots of properly brought up babies."

Jason asked curiously. "What's wrong with that?"

Merrill shrugged. "Absolutely nothing and absolutely everything."

He burst into laughter. Merrill stared at him, thinking how boyish his laughter was. He took such delight in so many things. He never seemed to notice he was an adult. He reminded her a bit too much of her father.

Merrill's childhood had been a back and forth existence of extremes. During the winter she'd lived a stable life of private schools, and tea parties with Nana. During the summer she had traveled with her parents in their old Volkswagen bus, following the

Grateful Dead. Not that her parents were irresponsible. They were just free spirits. She understood her father's behavior as a rebellion against his childhood. At times she even envied him, but she knew that wasn't for her. She had craved stability in her life. She needed to know what she would be doing from one minute to the next. She needed a plan to live her life.

Jason's laughter trailed away. "Aren't you going to meet this guy?"

"As soon as I get off the phone with the police." She noticed how his snug white t-shirt molded itself to his chest, revealing every taut muscle. Rutledge-Shelby wouldn't have tight muscles. She'd be surprised if he had any muscles at all. She didn't want a soft man. She wanted a man like Jason with laugh lines around his eyes. And muscles. She wanted a man who enjoyed his life. Rutledge-Shelby would be too busy keeping up with the Joneses.

"What are you doing?" Jason asked.

"Running a check on Violet and Marco."

He grinned at her. "Aren't you the suspicious one."

She loved the way he smiled. His teeth were so straight and white. "According to the contract they showed us, Miss Eulalie signed it the day she was buried. Doesn't that make you suspicious?"

"I was suspicious the minute they parked their van in front of the house." He filled a glass of water and drank from it, then filled it again and leaned against the counter, eyeing her.

The gleam in his eyes made her feel mushy inside, like he knew all her secrets. "Hopefully, in a few minutes we'll know if Violet and Marco are for real or not."

"Speaking about 'for real', what about that guy cooling his heels in the living room? Your grandma seems really anxious for you to meet him."

She rolled her eyes. "Be still my beating heart." Jason made her heart race. He made everything race.

"He could be a really nice guy."

She sighed. "Let me tell you about Carter Rutledge-Shelby."
And how very different he is from you.

"You haven't met him yet."

She smiled. "Nana is nothing if not consistent in her choices. Rutledge-Shelby's lineage probably goes all the way back to the Battle of Hastings. And he can document each and every one of his relatives with at least two volumes as large as an encyclopedia. He is of English descent. We Charlestonians revel in our English roots. We have overlooked the Revolutionary War, as much as we have the Civil War, simply because we have a knack for choosing the wrong side."

"What does this have to do with Mr. Shelby?"

She took a deep breath. "Let me finish. He probably works for a bank, but not in an important capacity. He sits in a big office and has an empty desk because he's nothing but window dressing. He plays golf with the bank's important customers. He belongs to the right country club, and he probably went to any one of five schools."

"Really! Name them."

She held up her hand and ticked off each finger. "Duke, Ole Miss, Vanderbilt, University of South Carolina, and if he didn't mind sweating, he might have gone to the Citadel. He has his suits custom-made, but nothing trendy like Armani or Boss. He wears the same style his father wore: conservative, probably grey or blue. And no power tie for him. He wants to appear as though he has nothing to prove. Right now, he is wearing khaki pants, a navy blue blazer with a gold crest on the pocket and a silk hankie strategically designed to look casual. A white Oxford cotton shirt, ironed within an inch of its life, with a bow tie. And he's carrying a white straw Panama hat."

"It's beige," Jason said.

"What?"

"The hat is beige. How do you know all this?"

"Because Mr. Rutledge-Shelby, above all else, is a follower of Southern tradition."

"I thought tradition died with the Civil War."

"Oh, no. The South just changed course." The South needed new blood, and Jason was just the type of person to invigorate it, she decided. As time went on, she found herself less and less skeptical of Jason. He seemed to have genuinely loved Miss Eulalie and was concerned that her only legacy would be as an eccentric crackpot.

Jason gripped the door frame and laughed. "You really know your South."

"I live it every day." Merrill turned with a flourish. Her contact suddenly came on the phone. He gave her run down of the information, and there was nothing improper or out of place. Merrill was still distrustful of Marco and Violet, and she wanted them out of the house. She hung up the phone and glanced at Jason. "Before I go out to meet Mr. Shelby, you and I need to make a decision about the designers."

"I want them out. They make me nervous. I know the dogs seem to like them, but I can't help feeling that they are too friendly with the dogs, like they have some other motive for being here."

"Other than the wrong date, this contract is binding. Their receptionist could have just made a mistake. I don't want to tie up any of Miss Eulalie's money in a lawsuit if we fire them without just cause. But I think we can postpone this until I figure out a way to get us out of the contract without costing us half of Psyche's money."

"Do you really think you can get us out of the contract?"

"Mr. Stavros, I've been told I can charm the sun from the sky."

"I bet you can."

He ran a finger along the line of her chin, and she shivered. That one little touch sent her into a spiral of wanton frenzy. She sternly brought herself under control. She couldn't go into the living room with her emotions unleashed. Her grandmother would spot an emotional tizzy a mile away, and then she would have too many questions to answer.

"I guess I better get this over." She turned toward the door.

***

Carter Rutledge-Shelby reeked of gentility. He gave her a courtly bow and handed her a huge bouquet of gardenias. *Hmmm,* she thought, *Nana must have been priming him for weeks.*

"For you." He gave her a charming, well-practiced smile.

"Thank you." Merrill delicately sniffed at the edge of the bouquet. "They're lovely." A little tingle went through her. The odd, uncomfortable sensation seemed to be at odds inside her. As a matter of fact, she loved the scent of gardenias, so why did these smell so strange? Not quite like stinkweed, but not like gardenias either. A headache formed, and she forced herself to smile.

"Your grandmother said you adore gardenias."

Merrill studied the sly smile on her grandmother's lips. "How sweet of her." She glanced at Jason. He seemed angry.

Nana slapped her lemon yellow gloves into the palm of her hand. "How could you let Eulalie sell her furniture?"

"She donated the proceeds to charity."

Blythe's lips thinned into a straight line. "I can't believe she did something so irrational."

Merrill spread her hands. "Miss Eulalie couldn't take them with her."

Nana's gray eyebrows hit her hairline. "What a vulgar thing to say, Merrill Prescott. I raised you better than that."

Merrill felt a little mean, but she apologized anyway. "Excuse me, Nana."

Blythe flicked her gloves at Jason. "I don't believe I've been properly introduced."

"This is Jason Stavros." Merrill turned to him and noticed how uncomfortable he looked. A wave of sympathy washed over her. Nana could intimidate God. "Jason, this is my grandmother, Blythe Harrington Prescott."

Jason wiped his hands on the seat of his jeans. "How do you do, ma'am." He held his hand out to her.

Blythe eyed him and then daintily shook two fingers. "You're not from around here, are you?"

"No, ma'am."

Blythe turned to Carter and dimpled. "Carter, I want to introduce you properly to my granddaughter."

Merrill couldn't believe they treated Jason like he was less then a servant. How rude. And Nana had the gall to scold Merrill.

"Merrill, dear," she motioned Carter over. "This is Carter Rutledge-Shelby of the Atlanta Rutledges. He's new to our city."

Jason covered his mouth with his hand and cleared his throat loudly. Merrill could see he was just as upset with Carter as he had been with Belle Boyd and J.D.

Merrill shook Carter's soft hand. "How do you do, Mr. Shelby?" Another odd, disturbing tingle went through her. Jason's touch had the ability to transport her. Carter's touch made her want to wash her hands with disinfectant.

"I used to believe Atlanta had the most beautiful women. Now I see I was wrong."

"Thank you," Merrill replied.

Nana smiled approvingly, reminding Merrill of a water mocassin ready to strike.

"Nana." Merrill tilted her head toward Jason.

Nana frowned, then grudgingly said. "Carter, this is Mr. Jason Stavros."

Jason held out his hand. "Of the Brooklyn Stavros'."

Merrill tried not to laugh. Carter's eyebrows rose so high on his forehead, they could have been singed by the heat of the sun. Merrill studied his blond hair, pale blue eyes and milky white skin. This was what came from hundreds of years of selective inbreeding among Southern families.

The two men shook hands. Carter acted as though his fingers were soiled.

Blythe hooked her arm through Carter's. "Carter just began working at National Bank and Trust. He's the director of Client Relations."

Carter blushed. "Your grandmother makes me sound more important than I really am. Sometimes I think I just play golf and tennis for a living."

"Do tell." Merrill couldn't resist her jab.

Jason smiled. "That's a nice jacket, Mr. Rutledge-Shelby."

"This old thing?" Carter replied. "It's my old fraternity jacket."

"And what school was that?" Merrill asked.

Carter brushed the crest on the pocket with his fingers. "Duke."

Merrill shot Jason a look and repressed her grin. "I never would have a guessed."

Carter's gaze bounced between Merrill and Jason, a quizzical expression on his face. "Am I missing something?"

Merrill dimpled at him. "Not at all Mr. Rutledge-Shelby. Not at all."

"Merrill," Nana snapped. "Stop playin' games."

Chastised, Merrill replied, "Yes, Ma'am. What brings you here?"

Blythe grabbed Carter's arm. "Carter and I came to ask you to dinner this evening. I'm introducing him around, trying to make him feel at home, and we want you to accompany us. I've made reservations at Broderick House."

Merrill tried not to faint. Broderick House was one of the most expensive restaurants in Charleston. When would Nana understand they were no longer wealthy?

"You are my guests tonight," Carter said.

Blythe patted his arm. "You are such a gentleman, Carter."

Merrill wondered where Nana had managed to find Carter Rutledge-Shelby. "Grandma, how did the two of you meet?"

"We were admiring the roses in White Point Garden with the Horticultural Society. I bought new orchids for the greenhouse, and he offered to carry them for me."

"Nana, you only live around the corner."

Carter favored Nana with an admiring smile. "No lady should carry anything, no matter how short the distance."

His solicitous manner made Merrill wonder what Carter was after. He didn't seem the type of man to marry a woman whose only asset was a pedigree. Merrill felt caught between a rock and a hard place. If she didn't meet them for dinner, she would look rude, and then she would have to deal with the wrath of Nana. "What time do you want me to meet you?"

"We have reservations for six o'clock," Blythe replied. "Be prompt, please." She tossed Carter a flirtatious look. "I wouldn't want Carter to get the idea we're not mannerly."

Jason opened the door for Nana and helped her down the stairs. Carter hung back. He took Merrill's hand and brought it to his lips, gently kissing it. He was smooth. "Until tonight. I do look forward to your company at dinner." He winked at her, and his eyes seemed to sparkle like jewels in the sun. How strange. She'd never seen the human eye do such a trick.

Dazed, Merrill watched Carter escort Nana down the walkway and turn toward her house.

***

Jason closed the door and turned to eye Merrill. "You don't seem too happy about this dinner."

Merrill sighed. "My grandmother is like a bulldozer wrapped in silk and Chanel No. 5. I feel like I've been fighting this subtle battle with her all my life. 'Don't be a lawyer. Get married. Have twenty-one kids. Meet the right man. Why do you want a career?' I have to go my own way, but she always makes me feel so guilty for fighting her, that she tires me out."

"You don't have to put up with it."

"She's my grandmother and I love her. I know in her heart she thinks she's doing what's right for me."

A hammering sounded from the next room.

"Violet and Marco," Merrill said as she headed toward the dining room. "I almost forgot about them."

Merrill walked down the hallway in front of him. She was smart, and he knew she would make the decorators' departure quick and painless.

As she moved ahead of him, he watched her hair, pulled into a pony tail, sway back and forth. Her butt wriggled enticingly. For one moment, she reminded him of the epitome of a fresh-faced, all-American girl. In the next moment, the luscious curves of her body conflicted with that wholesome image.

He wondered if Carter Rutledge-Shelby saw her in that way. Probably not. Rutledge-Shelby didn't have much depth to him, and that made Jason angry. Merrill needed a man who would appreciate her complexities, not someone who wanted a showpiece.

The decorators stood at the window overlooking the back yard, arguing in low voices. At Merrill and Jason's entrance, they whipped around, guilty smiles appearing.

Merrill got right to the point. "Marco and Violet. Right now is not a good time for you to be here."

"But, Miss Eulalie wanted us here," Violet cried.

"I know it was Miss Eulalie's wish to have you redecorate the house, but Jason and I need some time...."

Marco interrupted. "To mourn your loss."

"Exactly." Jason said with a smile.

Violet nodded solemnly. "I understand completely. You two should take comfort in each other."

Merrill glanced at Jason. "I'm glad you understand." Merrill bit the inside of her cheek, her lips quivering with amusement.

"Of course we understand," Violet patted Jason's shoulder. "Miss Eulalie told me how much the two of you meant to her and how much she wanted you to have time together to sort out your relationship."

Jason studied Violet's face. The woman looked so sincere, as though she'd just had this conversation with Eulalie. "Merrill and I just met. We have no relationship."

Violet grinned. "You can live a lot of life in a few minutes."

"If you say so," Jason replied.

With a coy smile, Violet said, "I'm wiser than I look."

Marco grabbed Violet. "We have to go." He tugged her out the door. "We'll see you later."

"Bye, you two lovebirds," Violet trilled.

Marco jerked her out the front door and it closed.

"Translate this last scene for me," Jason said to Merrill.

"I don't know. I was hoping you could tell me."

"I'm not as smart as I look."

Merrill shrugged. "Me, either."

Merrill started to giggle. Jason joined her. Soon, they were helpless with laughter. Jason draped an arm around Merrill, and she leaned into him. The subtle scent of her cologne reminded him of a new spring day right after a rain. Her body was so warm and inviting, his heart raced, and he wanted to hold her forever.

"Are we going to kiss now?"

"Seems like a good idea to me." His lips found hers. Her breath was sweet and minty. Her lips were soft. Tentatively, his tongue touched hers, and for an instant he realized he'd been wanting to do this forever. Her hands slid up his arm and entwined around his neck. He wanted to touch her all over.

Her body curled into his. Carter Rutledge-Shelby would never make the grade with Merrill. She needed more from a man than a pretty face, a bouquet of flowers and a few compliments. Rutledge-Shelby would never understand that Merrill's soul ran deep.

She moaned, pressing herself harder against him.

Something tugged at his pant leg. He opened one eye and glanced down, trying not to break the kiss. Buster's hot breath panted against Jason's knee. Then Buster barked and ran toward the back door and gently clawed at the threshold. That was Buster's sign. Kisses could wait. Buster had to go out.

***

Jason climbed the ladder, and set near the hole the extra boxes of nails the hardware company had delivered. Merrill, sitting on the slope of the roof, opened her toolbox. He couldn't believe she'd offered to help him finish the patching job.

"What part of your finishing school education taught you how to fix a roof?"

She glanced up at him. "What makes you think I went to finishing school?"

"Your grandmother looks like the type to make sure her granddaughter takes fan-twirling 101."

"Fan-twirling was an elective, and I chose eyelash batting instead." She batted her eyelashes at him.

He hadn't meant to sound so sarcastic, but the words had slipped out anyway. "That was out of line, wasn't it?"

"Yeah. But I was being polite." She ripped a loose shingle away from the edge of the patch. "For your information, I can cook and sew, and I can even type a hundred words a minute."

"I didn't think women like you cooked."

She glared at him. "Do you mean blondes like me? Or college educated blondes like me? Or blonde lawyers like me?"

"I'm digging myself a really deep hole here, aren't I?" A curl fell forward across her eyes. He wanted to push it back, remembering how soft her skin was, how sweet her cologne.

Merrill grinned at him. "So far, you're about waist deep."

"I get your point. You're not what I expected. Where did you learn all of these things?"

She sat on the roof and looked at him. "My parents liked to travel. When they needed a job, they could always find one at a truck stop—my mom as a cook and my dad as a handyman."

"Now why would your parents need to work?" Jason did some mental re-arranging. He liked the picture he'd already built of her in his mind, and he didn't like that fact she was smashing all his pre-conceived notions to bits.

"To eat, of course."

"You went to private schools and Harvard, yet your parents worked at truck stops? Please explain this to me."

"My parents are somewhat free-spirited, and Dad's way of rebelling was to live off the land, so to speak."

"Like hippies?"

She pointed a finger at him. "Bingo. Right down to the VW bus with a peace sign on the side and Grateful Dead bumper stickers."

Jason burst out laughing. "Your parents are hippies!" He couldn't believe this straight-laced woman came from such a peculiar background. He swiped a hand across his sweaty forehead. The humidity was getting to him, or maybe it was just the woman. "How did you end up living with your grandmother?"

"The evil baby fairies left me on the doorstep."

"That's not what I meant."

"My parents are terrific people, and I love them, but their lifestyle is just too erratic. That's how Nana ended up with me. Mom and Dad realized I needed structure in my life. I attended school in Charleston, living with Nana, and when school was out, my parents picked me up for a summer of wandering. I had the best of both worlds."

"I'll have to rethink my opinion of you." So she wasn't just fluff, and she wasn't a debutante. She was a sexy, intriguing, and intelligent woman. Everything he'd always wanted in a woman and had never seemed to find. If he was a smart man, he'd try to find a way to break the will just to get away from her. No matter how much he owed to Eulalie, he didn't think he could take being this close to Merrill for all the years to come.

She tilted her head at him. "Is that an apology?"

"Yeah, but I can't say the 'S' word. It's a guy thing."

"Saying your sorry isn't gender-specific, nor is roofing." She turned back to her task.

Jason felt like spit on the bottom of a sneaker. She hammered at the plywood patch. Serena would never have stopped by his office, much less joined him on a roof to help him. She wouldn't have wanted to mar the perfection of her manicure, or the softness of her hands.

Merrill's hands were large for a woman. Her long fingers were tipped with short-trimmed nails painted a pale pink. Despite the feminine concession, she looked strong and capable. Her breasts moved against the force of her hammering. They curved gently under the soft jersey of her t-shirt. No one on his crew had ever looked this good. Good enough to seduce.

What was Eulalie thinking when she insisted they share custody of the dog? Eulalie had said Kerry Blue Terriers were long-lived. He didn't know how he was going resist the subtle allure of her for the next ten years, or however long Psycho would be around. He didn't think he was going to make it through the next ten minutes. He helped her secure the plywood patch, hoping the extra exertion would exhaust him so that he'd sleep without dreaming. He didn't want a repeat of last night's extravaganza.

***

Jupiter mentally rubbed his hands together as he waited in the restaurant. He found Broderick House quaint and, for mortals, sophisticated. A man became jaded after naked nymphs had served him grapes. He hadn't realized how bored he'd become, or how weary. Merrill would spice up his life.

The door to the street opened, and Merrill entered. She wore a purple silk dress that draped over her bosom almost toga style. This woman had goddess-like class.

"Miss Merrill." He inhaled her fragrance. She was the loveliest creature since Marilyn Monroe, tragic girl. He'd always had a thing for blondes. "I'm so glad you're here."

"Where is my grandmother?"

"Your table is ready, sir." The waiter rushed over and escorted them to an intimate corner.

"My grandmother?" Merrill prompted again as the waiter snapped her napkin across her lap.

He heaved a dramatic sigh. "Blythe has abandoned me."

"You mean Nana stood you up?"

He gave her a huge grin. "I'm afraid so, but at least I have your beauty to console me."

"Mr. Rutledge-Shelby, we are not who my grandmother pretends to be."

"You're not two beautiful, intelligent, charming, well-mannered Southern ladies?" He gave her his best winning smile, a smile that would invite anyone to confide in him. He reached out to hold her hand, but she withdrew, and his feelings were hurt. How could she be so resistant to him? He needed some stronger magic. Beneath the cover of the table, he quietly snapped his fingers, and a box slid into his hand. Let her resist this. He slid the box into his pocket.

"The Prescott name is our only asset. Our treasury is empty."

"What a delightful way you put that, my dear." She was so charming, his heart ached.

"Carter, there is nothing delightful about poverty. If you're here hoping for a well-brought-up, wealthy Southern wife, you will have to look elsewhere."

"You are blunt, aren't you?"

"I don't want you wasting your time."

He took her hand and gently slid his thumb along her palm. "Nothing about you is a waste of time. I find you utterly enchanting."

"Thank you," she mumbled. For a second her shoulders slumped, and a look of defeat briefly crossed her face, like she was trying to let him down easy.

"If you don't mind my being so forward." He pulled a long thin jewelry box from his pants pocket, set it on the table between them, and opened it to reveal a platinum diamond bracelet. The diamonds sparkled in the candlelight. "These are the tears of the Goddess Ops. Legend states that for each God that she gave birth to, her tears would turn to diamonds. Any woman who wears this bracelet will find happiness in marriage and bear many children."

"What a lovely story." She stared, entranced, at the bracelet.

"I'm up on all the Roman legends." The legend was half correct. Actually, his father, Saturn had had the bracelet made to wear down the resistance of any mortal maiden when he wanted a little fun on the side. When Jupiter took control of the heavens, this was one of the benefits. With this bracelet on, Merrill would fall under his spell and into his bed for as long he wanted her.

He removed the bracelet from the box and wrapped it around her wrist.

"Carter, I cannot accept this. I hardly know you."

He sat back, waiting for the bracelet's magic to work. Merrill tugged at it, but it wouldn't come loose. She started scratching. "I hate to seem rude, but what is this made out of?"

"Platinum, of course. What else?" As though he would use something as common as gold.

"It's really itching. I've never had an allergic reaction to platinum before." She held her wrist up, scratching at her skin.

The platinum was turning black. Jupiter stared at her wrist. He didn't understand. This bracelet had never failed. He wanted to scream in outrage.

She worked the clasp open, and the bracelet fell away. Her skin had started to swell. "I don't want to be rude, but I think I need to go."

She stood up, gathered her purse, and left him in the restaurant as though he were nobody. No woman, goddess or mortal, had ever dared to treat him as nothing but an insignificant lackey!

He lifted his arms, and everyone in the restaurant froze in place. He walked out onto the street. Cars were stopped in the middle of the road. With a clenched fist, he threw back his head and let out a yell. The heavens rumbled.

With his rage dissipated, he snapped his fingers, and the world started again. He would have to think of something else. Some strange force was shielding Merrill from him. He would have to break it so he could have her.

Damn it! He needed to talk to Venus. She would know what to do.

But as much as his darling daughter adored him, he couldn't confide in her without letting her know his entire scheme. Venus would blab, and everyone would know his new policy was nothing but a sham.

Six

Dusk had fallen, and the day's heat had cooled. Ocean breezes ruffled the trees. Merrill let herself into the quiet house.

Psyche's Folly sniffed at her heels, and Merrill absently patted the dog. Psyche padded off, her nails clicking on the wood floors.

"Have a nice time?" Jason sat on the dark stairs leading to the second floor. Buster slept, curled up at his feet.

"Interesting." She sat next to him.

"How does a Southern gentleman date?"

"Southerners don't date. We court." Or in the matter of Carter, bribe. Her wrist still ached from the allergic reaction to the bracelet. She had even considered stopping at the Urgent Care Clinic, but half-way home the itching had finally abated.

"So did Rutledge-Shelby come up to snuff in the courting business?"

Merrill stretched. "He's amusing company."

"Only amusing?"

"He's a bit enthusiastic." Merrill had tried to be polite, but his too-smooth manners and odd way of saying things—as though he'd spent hours watching movies about the South—had bothered her. There was something fake about Carter. His words were too sincere, his actions too smooth, as though he were trying to consummate a deal. "He's almost too Southern."

"How can someone be too Southern?"

Merrill leaned her elbows on her knees trying to analyze
Carter. "I can't quite put my finger on it. I feel like he's read *Gone
With The Wind* one too many times." She shook her head. Why was
Jason interrogating her?

"Does that mean you won't be going out with him again?"

"We never discussed it. I had an allergic reaction to this
bracelet he tried to give me, and I had to leave." Was Jason jealous?
How could he be? This was getting too strange. She didn't like
strange. Strange made her nervous.

Jason jumped up and paced back and forth. "He gave you a
bracelet? That's pretty quick on only one meeting."

"You don't know the half of it. A big, gaudy diamond
bracelet set in platinum. I've never had a reaction to platinum
before."

"I thought every woman liked diamonds."

"No. Some of us like turquoise, or lapis lazuli, or jade."

"I would have thought you would have more expensive tastes.
I would give you sapphires."

Merrill stared at him. "Unless they came from your heart,
they would mean nothing to me. Carter's came from a region lower
on his anatomy."

"That's pretty harsh."

Merrill cupped her chin in her hand. "Carter has lots of words
and little meaning." Merrill frowned. This conversation was so off.
She stood, hands on hips. Buster stirred and moved away. "Why are
you so concerned about whom I go out with?"

"Because..." He grabbed her shoulders and pulled her to him,
kissing her. His lips moved over hers, taking everything he
could—deeply, thoroughly and passionately.

Merrill thought her knees had turned to butter. She almost
slid out of his arms, so great was her shock. Yet, an electrified thrill
started at her lips and tingled its way to her toes. His lips were soft
yet demanding. His tongue swept over hers in a promise of more
delights to come. He smelled like soap and sea breezes. His body

was hard and muscular. Crushed against him, his strength engulfed her.

She curled her fingers through his unruly hair. With her mouth pressed against his, she was loathe to let him go. She felt secure, protected and wanted. For a moment, she didn't want him to stop. Then she pushed him away.

"What do you think you're doing?" she sputtered.

"I don't know, but a kiss seemed to be appropriate." He stepped back.

"Well, it wasn't. You have to stop kissing me."

"I didn't see you objecting."

"I didn't want to be rude." She stomped up the stairs to her room, more angry with herself than with him. His kiss was wonderful, and she was annoyed that she found herself attracted to a him.

She showered and pulled on her nightgown. With the balcony doors open to the night breezes, she flopped on the bed. Psyche and Buster sat on the floor at the bedside looking at her, their ears tilted in her direction and their tails wagging, as though expecting a commentary on the kiss.

Merrill wanted to throw a pillow at them. "I didn't start it; he did."

They barked.

"I didn't know what to do," Merrill objected. "He laid a lip-lock on me so fast I couldn't say no."

Their heads bobbed up and down as though agreeing with her.

"I'm really not attracted to him." Had she said that more for herself, or for them? From the expressions on the dogs' faces, they obviously didn't believe her. "We're so different. He's so outgoing. I don't know if you have noticed, but I tend to be a little reserved."

The dogs looked at each other. They blinked at the same time, and Merrill wanted to push them out the door. She didn't need two dogs to talk to. She needed a friend, and the only friend she could think of was Lula, who was probably on a date. Lula had a black book that was bigger than the phone book.

Merrill was in this mess alone. She had a lot of thinking to do. Jason was never far from her thoughts, and she didn't like that. He was taking up too much of her brain space. Why did she get stuck being a guardian to a dog? Merrill longed for the time when her life wasn't so complicated, or strange.

And the worst of it all, she didn't even want to go to sleep. The minute her head hit the pillow, she was going to have another one of those sex fantasy dreams. For all she knew, she'd be running naked in the meadow with Jason following her wearing nothing but a smile.

***

Venus and Eulalie tossed their tennis rackets onto the chairs. Cupid was slumped in a chair. "What's the matter, Cupie?"

"I've never been fired before."

"They didn't fire us. They just told us we weren't needed right away."

Cupid glanced at his mom. "Hello, earth to Venus. We were fired." He turned to Eulalie. "Weren't we?"

Eulalie grinned. "You were fired."

"Why?" Venus asked. "We didn't even get a chance to do anything."

Eulalie produced the contract and showed it to Venus. "See that. You dated the contract the day my mortal remains were buried."

Venus frowned. "But that was the date I made the contract." She had been so careful. She had even made sure the contract sounded like a real contract. She'd studied dozens of them before finding the right one.

Eulalie rubbed her forehead. "Oh, Venus."

"What did I do wrong?" Venus stared at the contract.

Eulalie patted her on the shoulder. "It's a good thing you're pretty, dear. You should have changed the date to an earlier one. There is no way I could sign this when my body was six feet under."

"Oh! I didn't think of that." Next time, she would get Daniel Webster to go over her contracts. Danny snook-ums always knew what to do.

Cupid chuckled. "We know, Ma. That's okay."

Venus nodded. "We still have Plan B." She sort of liked Plan B.

"Mom," Cupid said, "I'm not going to be a dog. You'd better come up with Plan C."

"Plan C involves a hurricane, and they just had one."

"Plan C sounds good to me." Cupid had a pleading look in his eyes.

"But, Cupid," Venus objected, "B comes before C in the alphabet. Even I know that."

"I'm going to be a schnauzer, aren't I?"

"Not exactly."

"What exactly? A hound dog?"

Venus shook her head. "You're going to be Buster. And I'm going to be Psyche's Folly." A mirror popped up in front of her face, and she preened.

Cupid groaned. Eulalie burst out laughing. "I think I'll head home. I can see you two have everything under control."

Venus trilled, "We always do."

***

By the next afternoon, Jason and Merrill had finished working on the roof. Jason glanced around at the work they'd accomplished, satisfied that the patch would keep out the rain until his custom-ordered materials arrived, and he could repair the roof properly.

Late in the afternoon, just as they were putting their tools away, a delivery van pulled into the driveway.

"What do they want?" Jason sat back on his heels and stared down at the van.

"I'd better go see." Merrill wiped her hands on her jeans, moved sideways toward the ladder, and descended with Jason following right behind.

"You stay, I'll go." He needed to get away for a few minutes. Every move she made reminded him of the soft caress of her body against his. Her clean fresh scent tickled his nose. Merrill had invaded his life. He wanted to go back a week into the past when

Eulalie was still alive, and the first time he had felt in control of his destiny since the divorce.

He signed for the heavy box. Merrill's name was neatly typed on the outside.

"Merrill," he called up to her. "You have a present."

She scrambled down as the van backed out of the driveway.

The box was probably from lover boy, and he wondered what was inside. Merrill took the box from him and went into the house. She set it on the kitchen table. With a knife, she opened the packing to reveal another box inside.

The box inside was wrapped in shiny gold paper with a silver bow.

"What do you think is inside?" Merrill asked as she studied the large box.

"A bomb from J.D. and Belle."

"That's pretty messy. And not Belle's style. She's sneaky." She tore open a card and read it. An odd look passed over her face. "Carter Rutledge-Shelby. I think he's trying to buy me."

"Open it up," Jason urged. "Let's see what his offer is."

The offer was a black sable coat.

"Oh, my God." Merrill stared at the box.

Jason was prepared to go back to disliking Merrill, but a look of total horror spread across her features.

She bent over the box and started to cry. "Those poor animals."

Not the reaction he'd been expecting. Serena would have been doing back flips over such an expensive gift. Another addition to her double-digit collection of dead animal pelts.

Tears streamed down Merrill's face. "Do you know how they kill those poor things? How could he?" She stood up and flipped the lid back over the coat. "Get this thing out of my sight. How could he believe I would accept something created from the suffering of other creatures! For nothing more than the sake of vanity."

"What are you going to do with it?" Jason wanted to comfort her. Her distress touched him.

"I'm sending it back to Van Horn's." She marched over to the phone and picked it up. Jason listened in as she spoke to the store and demanded they send a messenger to pick up the coat. When Merrill hung up, she glared at Jason. "When they come, you handle it."

"Why should I handle it? You handle it."

Her lips quirked like a smile was being born. "You just want to see me lose my cool, don't you?"

He grinned at her.

***

While Jason waited for the messenger from Van Horn's, Merrill went to her bedroom to call Carter. She fumed with anger. Even though the business day was almost over, she hoped he would be in his office. The receptionist said he wasn't in, and she had no idea where he was. He wasn't he at the country club, nor on the golf course. He wasn't anywhere.

How dare he? Did he think she was a piece of property to be bartered and bought with a diamond bracelet and a coat? Her grandmother had a lot of explaining to do. Even Nana wouldn't approve of the coat.

What would he send next? A car? A house? A vacation in the Bahamas? Didn't Carter understand, she wasn't the kind of person to be bribed? She wasn't impressed with possessions.

Why did Nana expect her to marry someone as lame and boring as Carter? Just because he had a big piggy bank didn't mean he was what Merrill wanted. She wanted a real man. A man who could laugh at her jokes and at himself. A man who could almost say the 'S' word. Someone like Jason.

She dropped the phone, startled. Jason. Her palms started sweating, and her stomach clenched into knots. She was in love with Jason. She sat down hard on a chair. She couldn't be in love with him. He was a client. She wasn't even sure he liked her. He seemed to be put off by her background, by her schooling, and by her name. She laughed. All those years of her grandmother telling her these elements were her three greatest assets, and the man she'd come to care for didn't give a hoot. Sometimes, life had a bizarre and twisted sense of humor.

Nana would keel over. Jason was not the kind of man she envisioned as husband material for Merrill. He didn't belong to a country club. He didn't play golf. He didn't wear custom-made clothes. He was just all wrong. Nana would never approve.

Wait a second, Merrill thought. *This is my life. Not Nana's.* If she wanted to be in love with Jason, she would be in love with Jason. And no one would stop her. Well, maybe Jason could. He was the obstacle, and Merrill didn't know how to get around him.

***

Jason guarded the fur coat. Despite Merrill's reaction to it, it was still an expensive item, and he wouldn't be comfortable until the messenger from Van Horn's took control of it.

Merrill returned to the kitchen. From the look on her face, he could tell she hadn't found Rutledge-Shelby. "No luck in finding the guy?"

"He's not anywhere." Merrill went to the stove. "As though he just disappeared off the planet. What are you boiling?"

"I'm making water for tea."

She glanced at him. "You drink tea?"

"Blame Eulalie. She corrupted me. She always felt that things looked better after a good, strong cup of tea." He reached for the tea cannister. The moment he touched it, a vision of Eulalie appeared. She was pouring a cup for him and telling him that he would fall in love again, and the next time would be forever.

Merrill sat down at the table, pushing the box away from her with a look of distaste. Jason took the box and stored it in the pantry. When he returned, Merrill thanked him.

Jason made the tea. Merrill rubbed the back of her neck. He could see she was very tense. He wanted to ease the lines of tension from her face, but all he could offer was the tea, sweetened with honey, and served in Eulalie's favorite Chinese cups.

Jason handed Merrill her cup. She sipped the hot tea and smiled at him. "I would think," she said, "a man would find out how a woman feels about things like this before making such a grand gesture."

"From the dawn of time, men have always assumed women would appreciate whatever little gesture they offered."

Merrill slanted a glance at him. "Do you feel like that?"

His heart did a huge lurch. "Once I did, a long time ago. But I learned the hard way that women are not so easily persuaded."

"I detect a note of bitterness in your voice."

He sipped his own tea. "Personal experience."

"Don't leave me hanging. I'm dying to know the most intimate details of your life." She put a hand on his.

Her touch was fire on the surface of his skin. "My ex-wife took me for a ride."

"I didn't know you were married."

"A long time ago." A time he'd rather forget.

Buster and Psycho entered the kitchen. Buster sat down next to Jason, and Jason gently tugged his ears. Buster shook his head. Psycho lay down in front of the stove and seemed to be staring at her reflection in the glass. She tilted her head back and forth as though admiring herself.

"The divorce obviously was not amicable."

"That's the understatement of the year." How did he explain Serena. Did he want to?

"Are you still in love with her?"

He exploded, "God, no."

Buster barked and wagged his tail. Buster couldn't stand her, either. He nuzzled Merrill's knee.

"That woman wanted to send my dog to dog summer camp."

"Dog's have summer camps?"

"The pampered pooches of the rich and shameless do. What are they going to do? Take the dogs on canoeing trips? I can just picture all these dogs gathered around the campfire singing about Bingo, the dog."

Merrill laughed. "I went to camp once, and only once."

"You're not built for the great outdoors, are you?"

"I love the outdoors. I envisioned nights around the campfire, singing songs and roasting marshmallows. But Nana's choice of summer camp entailed proper fork placement and the dainty art of eating canapes."

"Did you get dirty?"

Merrill shook her head. "We never saw the outdoors. We had maid service. Maid service, for heaven's sakes! I wanted to put snakes in my roomies' beds."

"You sound quite the tomboy." A picture of her sitting on the roof hammering away appeared in his mind.

"I don't think I was a tomboy. My parents taught me to appreciate nature, and nature gives Nana hives." She sipped at her tea. "That was very smart of you."

"What?"

"The old get-Merrill-to-talk-about-herself trick, so you don't have to reveal any of your secrets. I want to know about you, and all we seem to talk about is me."

Because he wanted to know everything about her. "In a nutshell. My life was simple. I married and my life became complicated. I got a divorce and my life became simple again." He shrugged. "That's pretty much it."

"At this moment, do you consider your life simple?"

How was he going to answer her question? "I have my work. I have Buster, but I've also inherited a dog and a blonde lady lawyer. My life is slowly becoming complicated again."

"How do you feel about that?"

"My best friend died. My house has a hole in the roof. I've been insulted, accused of fraud, and I have the oddest feeling that this is some big cosmic joke."

Buster barked and put a paw over his nose. Where did he learn that trick? Jason had the oddest sensation the dogs were eavesdropping. Psycho was still looking at herself in the glass door of the oven, but her ears flicked at Jason and Merrill. Buster eyed Jason as though he understood every word Jason had said.

"I think I know how you feel. Confidentially, I've met the man of Nana's dreams, and I can't stand him."

"That's too bad." Boy, did he sound insincere. He was also elated. He'd been thinking of Rutledge-Shelby as competition. Knowing the other man was out of the game gave Jason pause. Merrill could now be his.

Wait, he had no idea how she felt about him. Yet she had kissed him, and he would never forget the jolt of passion he'd felt at the touch of her lips. Her mouth was perfect. She had pouty, velvety lips that could make a man forget about everything except for kissing her, tasting her, making love to her.

He was becoming aroused. God, he wanted her. He wanted her in his bed, and in his life the same way she was taking over his heart and his head. The last few days he'd thought of little else but Merrill. He hadn't known he could feel so strongly for a woman again.

"Jason?" Merrill asked. "Are you all right? You look a little flushed. Are you coming down with something?"

He mentally shook himself and brought himself back from his musings. "Too much sun." Too much Merrill. "Maybe I'm just hungry. Dinner would help. What do you want?"

Psycho made an odd noise, and he stared at her. It almost sounded as though she were laughing. He'd never been laughed at by a dog before.

"What has gotten into those two dogs?" Merrill said.

"I have no idea. They are acting very undoglike."

"Do you think they've been possessed?" Merrill laughed. "We can have a doggie exorcism."

Buster jumped to his feet and, with Psyche in tow, rushed out of the kitchen, both of them yipping.

"What's gotten into them?" Merrill said, eyebrows raised.

"You'd think they understood every word we've been saying."

The front doorbell rang. Jason jumped to his feet. Finally, the messenger had arrived, and he could be rid of that damn fur coat.

He looked out the peephole and saw it was Rutledge-Shelby. Instead of opening the door, he went back to the kitchen and said to Merrill, "It's the great fur coat hunter. Do you want to talk to him? Or shall we just ignore him?" The doorbell sounded again.

Merrill went to the pantry and took out the box. "I want to give him a piece of my mind." She marched to the front door, the box clasped in front of her.

Her little butt swayed back and forth. Jason could feel the tension radiating off her. Damn, did she look sexy. Rutledge-Shelby was in for a bad time, and Jason wanted to see it.

Merrill opened the door, shoved the box at him and said, "Furs are dead." She slammed the door and leaned against it, staring at Jason. "Do you think he caught the hint?"

"I did."

The doorbell rang again. Merrill opened the door, and with her hands on her hips, glared at Carter.

A gentleman would leave. Hell, Jason was no gentleman. He was going to stay and watch the fireworks. The dogs came and sat on either side of him, watching Merrill and Rutledge-Shelby, their eyes alert and their ears pitched forward as though they were intensely interested in what was going to happen next.

***

Jupiter looked at the box in his hand. He didn't understand. This coat had more magic woven into the pelts than any other spell he'd ever cast before. And it didn't seem to work.

Merrill glared at him. "I do not believe in murdering animals for their fur."

Jupiter stared at her. "But every woman wants a fur coat." He glanced at the dogs sitting next to Jason, and he couldn't believe it when the dark one stuck its tongue out at him. Then the two dogs pivoted and ran away.

"Not this woman," Merrill replied.

Jupiter thought she was magnificent in her outrage. Her breasts heaved, her breath came in sharp gusts. Her cheeks were flushed, and her eyes sparkled. He knew it. She had all the pent-up passion of a cyclone, and he wanted it. "Forgive me, Merrill. I should have known commonplace gifts would never impress you."

"Carter," Merrill said, leaning forward slightly, "I can't be bought."

"I know that now." He smiled at her and shifted the box to one arm, whipping out a piece of paper with an incantation he'd stolen from Merlin just before Venus put him in that tree. "I wrote you a poem. If you would invite me in, I'd like to read it to you."

Merrill took the paper, folded it and put it back in his pocket. "Carter, as sweet as the gesture may be, I'm not interested. Please relay the message to my grandmother."

"Thank you, and have a nice day," Jason said as he closed the door.

Jupiter stared at the closed door and grinned. *Hot damn, this was exciting.* He hadn't had a woman this contentious since Europa.

Okay, Jupiter thought, *back to the drawing boards.* He would have to up the stakes. He would have Merrill Prescott. He didn't know when, and he didn't know how. Eventually he would have her because he was Jupiter: King of the Gods, Master of Destiny, Ruler of All He Surveyed.

Gods, he was impressed with himself.

Seven

While Merrill caught up on some of her paperwork, Jason spent the evening attempting to work up an estimate for his next project, the renovation of a local church. Even with the plans spread out in front of him, he couldn't concentrate. His thoughts kept drifting back to Merrill.

Finally, he gave up on the estimate and went to bed, where he spent the night tossing and turning, his dreams again filled with erotic images of him and Merrill making love. As the sun crested the horizon he gave up trying to sleep and decided a long jog was just what he needed to wear his libido out.

When he set out on his run, he admitted that the mornings were the hardest for him. This was the time he missed Eulalie the most. They had spent each morning sharing breakfast and the newspaper, talking about each others' plans for the day.

After he returned from his jog, he stopped in the kitchen before washing up. The newspaper lay on the kitchen table in front of William. William sipped orange juice and read.

"Morning, William."

"Good morning, sir. I have a favor to ask."

"Shoot," Jason said.

"Until the house is back to being normal, there is really nothing for me to do. Do you mind if I take a few weeks and visit my daughter?"

"Sure. Do you want me to drive you to the airport?"

William shook his head. "No, I like driving, and the trip gives me time to myself. I'll be fine, but thank you."

"No problem."

William continued, "I had a phone call from the girls, and they say they're fine, and they'll be heading back whenever you want them."

"When you're back from your daughter's, we'll decide on what to do next."

William left the table. A few minutes later, Jason heard the old Rolls Royce start up and purr down the driveway. For a moment he felt strange with William gone. He was now totally alone with Merrill.

Jason sat at the table and folded the paper back to the first page. He choked on his orange juice.

In glorious color on the front page was a picture of Jason and Merrill. Jason stood just behind her as they studied the hole in the roof, a scowl on his face that would frighten Satan himself. CRAZY SOCIALITE LEAVES MUTT MILLIONS. And underneath, RELATIVES VOW TO SEEK SANITY HEARING.

Merrill entered the kitchen. "I see you're reading that trashy rag." She looked luminous and all-out sexy with her blonde hair in ripples about her shoulders. She wore a prim straw hat, a silvery colored skirt that ended just below her knees, and a matching blouse.

Jason pushed the paper away. "I'm not reading this crap."

"You'd better, because you and I will have to defend Miss Eulalie in the competency hearing. And if you don't know what the other side is saying about you, you can't defend yourself properly."

Jason pulled the paper back. "You've read this already?"

"Over my coffee." She poured herself a fresh cup.

"How did this get in the paper?"

"Keep reading." Her mouth was tight and drawn.

The more he read, the more a chill grew around his heart. He could understand why Merrill was disturbed. Her entire family life for the last half century had been dissected. Everything from her father's anti-war and civil rights activities to the fact that her parents weren't married. Every detail of how the family lost their money had been thoroughly scrutinized. Even Merrill's academic career had been put under the microscope. The results were not pleasant, and the implications were more than disturbing.

Stunned, Jason reread the money part. He couldn't believe it. So she wasn't rich. He almost felt sorry for her. She walked around acting like her family had money, but, according to the article, she was pretty damn poor. The article went into extreme detail over how her uncle had lost the family fortune. The reporter had enjoyed tearing the Prescott family apart.

Jason's divorce from Serena and his somewhat wayward childhood had also been investigated. How the hell had the reporter found out about his teen-age escapade with the Fifth Street Lords and his one and only arrest for stealing hubcaps? His juvenile record was supposed to be sealed. So someone must have been talking to Serena. The leak had her fingerprints all over it.

He clenched his hands, trying to control his rage. Even his parents' quiet, middle-class lives has been pulled apart, including his dad's IRS audit which had led to an investigation of his mother's day care center. The fact that the IRS investigation had eventually exonerated his parents was not mentioned.

He flipped to the next page. A picture of Belle Boyd, looking prim and virginal, peered back at him. He read her interview and thought he would throw up. The woman was a leech in white gloves and a designer suit. Obviously money could buy sympathy, and on her home turf, she'd bought a lot.

He wished he had a puppy to paper-train. He would start the lessons with this trash. That was all it was good for.

Merrill watched him. "Not pretty."

"Can we sue them?"

"Is anything of what they've said about you untrue?"

"No."

"There's nothing false about my family, either, so we can't sue them. And Psyche's Folly is news. Miss Eulalie's will is public record."

"Damn it all."

Merrill shrugged. "It'll blow over. Something new will replace it."

"How can you be so calm?" He wanted to rip the paper and the reporter to shreds. He wanted to put out a contract on Belle Boyd and J.D. Their comments on Eulalie's sanity galled him. Didn't the reporter see that they were greedy and unethical?

"Because it's Sunday, and I'm on my way to church. And the fact that my grandmother will let me know exactly how she feels means there is nothing I can do or say that will equal the rampage that she will go on. So I have decided that for these last few minutes of life, I will think happy thoughts."

"You'd think they'd check with us first."

"Oh no. Then they might get another side of the story, one that isn't so glamorous or sensational."

As casually as he could, Jason folded the newspaper to hide the story. Then he folded it again to hide their front-page picture. "I'll see you when you get back."

"You're welcome to come along."

"Thanks, but no thanks." He hadn't been in church since just before the divorce. "I need to check that roof. The news says another storm is going to be here tonight."

"I should be home later in the afternoon. I'm having brunch with my grandmother and Mr. Rutledge-Shelby."

"I thought you were done with him." Jealousy rose in Jason.

"Nana hasn't received the news yet."

She stood, picked up her purse and walked out the back door, leaving Jason alone with the newspaper and his thoughts.

***

After church, Merrill parked her car in the driveway. She had managed to beg off from brunch with Carter and her grandmother by saying that the newspaper article had left her feeling depressed, and she needed to be alone. Jason had covered the roof patch with a bright-blue tarp, the ends flapping slightly in the breeze. Clouds had darkened the horizon, and the humidity had jumped thirty percent in the last hour.

She got out of her car and slammed the door, looking around for Jason. He was nowhere in sight.

"Hey, lady," a voice called.

Merrill whirled around. A little boy, maybe nine years old, stood against the bushes, almost invisible in his dark green pants and blue and green shirt. In his arms he held a wriggling puppy the color of rust.

"Hello there," Merrill replied. "Can I help you?"

"Are you the lady with the rich dog?"

"Yes, I guess so." She hadn't thought about the dog being rich.

The little boy walked up to her and held the puppy out to her. Huge tears rolled down his freckled cheeks.

"What's wrong?" Merrill asked.

He started to sob. "Dad says to get rid of her." The squirming puppy tried to lick Merrill's hand. "We can't take care of her no more. If you don't take her, we'll have to take her to the pound. They kill puppies at the pound." His narrow shoulders shook. "You have money. She's just little. She won't eat much."

The dog was fat and sassy and looked well-cared for. Without thinking about it, Merrill took the puppy. Its fur was soft and sleek, and its butterball shape made Merrill want to cradle the little thing in her arms. The boy ran away before she could ask the puppy's name.

Psyche's Folly galloped across the grass, Buster on her heels. Psyche sniffed at the puppy. The puppy squirmed harder trying to get down. Merrill set the animal on the ground and watched as Psyche immediately took over, nuzzling it.

"What have we here?" Jason asked as he walked up.

"A new addition to the family."

Jason knelt down and gently stroked the puppy's head. "She's not very old." The puppy rolled over on her back and wriggled in ecstacy. "Did you find her?" Jason tickled her exposed belly and chuckled as the puppy licked his fingers.

Merrill knelt down on the ground next to him, marveling that he could be so gentle. "A little boy brought her. He seemed to think we'd have room."

Jason chuckled. "I think, for this one, we can make a spot."

"From the size of those paws, I think this puppy is going to need her own house."

Jason examined the puppy's paws. "You may be right."

Merrill watched him. How could that woman leave him? What was wrong with his ex-wife? Jason was funny and intelligent. He was good with animals and liked old people.

The puppy barked joyfully and suddenly bolted upright, racing away. Psyche followed. Buster sat down to watch the antics.

Jason stood and brushed grass from his jeans. "You never got around to telling Belle Boyd and J.D. exactly how you wanted Eulalie's shelter to operate. I think we just received our first tenant."

Merrill smiled as the puppy rolled in the grass, obviously happy. "I'm sure they'll find a way to make the shelter seem like an old woman's nonsense."

"Knowing how you feel, are you going to be able to defend her?"

"Did I give you the impression that I didn't support Miss Eulalie's wishes? Last wishes are sacred. If Miss Eulalie wanted to stand in her front yard and burn her money in a bonfire, I would defend her right to do so."

Jason glanced at her. "This battle is going to get uglier, isn't it?"

Merrill sighed. "I don't think ugly is the right word." She didn't want to think about the future. She wanted to think about now, about Jason.

"Good," he said, "Let's get our new child settled."

Merrill grinned at him, a strange warmth invading her at the way he said 'our child'. What a delicious thought. "You make me feel like we're foster parents."

"In a strange, four-legged kind of way, we are."

The sun shone off his black hair. His dark, unfathomable eyes held a mischievous glint she found incredibly attractive. Something fun and absolutely wicked surrounded him. He was the kind of man her grandmother warned her to stay away from. She'd once told Merrill to get a man she could tame and manipulate. A man who wouldn't cause trouble or chase after other women.

Watching Jason walk away from her, with his tight rear-end and long, muscular legs, she knew he was nothing but trouble. Her mother and father would love Jason. He was working-class, down-to-earth, and didn't have a pretentious bone in his body. The more time she spent with him, the more appealing he became. Daddy would be proud of her. Grandmother would have a heart attack.

Jason slammed open the door to the kitchen. The puppy wriggled in his arms. While he went to find food for the puppy, Merrill made them sandwiches.

The phone rang. Merrill answered it. Her grandmother was on the other end, raging. "Did you read the society page?"

Merrill never read the society page. "Not yet."

"Read it. Having your picture splashed all over the front page was bad enough, but having you as the hot topic of gossip on the society page is going to give me a stroke. Prescotts, as far back as the Twelfth Century, are rolling over in their graves."

"Nana, I'll call you back later." She hung up the phone and flipped open the paper. A picture of her from some long ago function graced the society page.

She slammed the newspaper down just as Jason walked into the kitchen, the puppy scrambling after him. He held a dish of food which he set on the floor. The puppy greedily shoved his nose into the kibble.

"Can you believe that?" Merrill stormed. "Who the hell do those yellow journalists think they are? They don't know the first thing about my private life." She punched a finger at the article. "Cohabitating. They have us *cohabitating.*"

Jason removed the paper from her hands and put it on the floor. He set the puppy on top of the paper. "This is all these articles are worth. Go ahead, Annie, do you business."

The puppy's tale wagged uncontrollably.

Merrill started to laugh. "Annie?"

Jason gestured at the puppy. "She's red. She's orphaned. She has great big eyes."

"Her eyes have pupils."

He grinned. "Use your imagination." He picked up the puppy and stroked her fur.

The puppy was so tiny, she fit in his hand. Jason smoothed the red fur, and Merrill thought he was a man who needed children. He'd make a great father.

Merrill took the puppy from him. Little Annie tucked her head against Merrill's neck, and an odd sensation swept over her. For the first that she could ever remember, she wondered what it would be like to hold her own baby. What would it be like to hold Jason's baby? That whole idea threw her for a loop. She studied the puppy, whose eyes closed into sleep. She gently cradled Annie in her lap. When she looked up, Jason was gone.

Carefully, without disturbing the slumbering pup, she reached for the newspaper, opened it back to the society page and finished reading.

***

Jupiter stared at Blythe Prescott, seated across the table from him, trying not to let the flames shoot out of his ears. The old woman droned on and on about Charleston history as though he didn't already know. He'd been there. He'd caused the settlement of Charleston to happen. In fact, if he'd been alert over Neptune's recent activities, the last hurricane wouldn't have happened. Charleston was one of his favorite places.

116   J. M. Jeffries

Blythe took dainty bites of her lunch. Jupiter had the woman in the palm of his hand. But how to manipulate her into helping him win the granddaughter? That was who he really wanted.

"Carter, dear." Blythe patted his hand. "You haven't answered my question."

"What question? I was thinking about Merrill." And how disappointed he was she had decided to cancel lunch.

"Merrill is distracted by her job. I would really like to find a way to ease her worries. She works so hard."

Even Jupiter could take a hint. "You mean you want a rich husband for her, so she doesn't have to work."

Blythe fluttered her hand. "Was I bein' so forward?"

Jupiter took her hand. "No my dear. Two great minds just thinking alike."

Blythe giggled. "You mean to say, you like my granddaughter."

"Very much." Jupiter wanted her so badly, he could barely contain his passion. That woman needed a good night of his special brand of lovemaking. He was good enough that she would never be satisfied with a mortal man for the rest of her life.

Blythe patted her lips daintily with the cloth napkin. "You must escort her to my cotillion. That will be your chance to show her the sincerity of your feelings."

What the hell did this old woman think he'd been doing? Jupiter hadn't planned to wait around that long, but for Merrill Prescott the Fourth, he would.

"Now," Blythe said, "we must plan. Let me say that furs and diamonds are not Merrill's cup of tea. You must think simple for her. Wildflowers from the meadows. Organic honey." Blythe sighed. "I know her father's evil influence on her has been so hard to break. But I'm sure you can figure out a way. You're such an intelligent man."

A waiter approached. "More water?" He held out the pitcher.

The pitcher slipped and hit the edge of the table. Water landed in Jupiter's crotch. He barely stopped himself from turning the waiter into a toad.

"I'm so sorry, sir." A small smile hovered on the waiter's lips. "Please forgive me. I don't know what happened." The waiter offered his arm towel for Jupiter to mop up the mess.

Jupiter accepted the towel. "It's not a problem. After all, water isn't going to hurt anything." He had to admit, the ice-cold water had dampened his ardor for the moment.

***

Venus couldn't stop giggling. "Did you see his face? That was more fun than being a dog and sticking my tongue out at him." She always loved pulling a fast one on the old guy. As she walked across the marble floor of her mansion, she turned back into her old self. The waiter uniform disappeared. Her toga snapped to attention and began to wrap itself around her body.

Cupid stared at her. "How did you get away with it? Where did you put the ring?"

She raised the hem of her toga and lifted her foot for him to see. The ring encircled her big toe. "Everyone thinks I'm nothing but a pretty face and a great set of hooters."

Cupid was shocked. "Hooters! Where did you hear that word?"

"I've been watching television. It's very educational. I think more gods should watch." She snapped her fingers, and a glass of wine appeared. "Daddy is truly enthralled with Merrill."

"I don't blame him. She's beautiful and brainy."

"With a great set of hooters."

"I can't agree more."

Venus fluttered her eyelashes at him. "I'm shocked, Cupie. How can say such things in front of your mother?"

"You taught me everything I know, Ma."

She erupted into giggles. Venus loved being Venus.

Eight

Merrill burned the newspaper. She set fire to it in the living room fireplace and sat back on her heels to watch the flames curl and blacken the pages.

Psyche, Buster and Annie watched her. Psyche was black. Buster had white spots and Annie was red. They looked a mismatched family.

"I know freedom of the press is a good thing," she told the dogs. Buster's ears poked forward. "But those people had no right to expose my whole life to the city of Charleston." Buster barked. Annie's tail wagged furiously.

"And," Merrill continued, "did you read that drivel they wrote about Jason?" Psyche yawned and dropped down to the ground, resting her head on her paws. "Can you believe the way they smeared Miss Eulalie's good name?"

Anne rolled over on her back, paws in the air.

"If it wasn't against the law, I'd have a bonfire on the lawn, and I'd burn every newspaper and tabloid in the city."

"And," Jason said from behind her, "I'd provide the matches."

Startled, Merrill jumped to her feet. "How much of that conversation did you hear?"

Jason leaned against the door frame. He wore a white t-shirt that hugged every muscle of his upper body. His tool belt was slung low over his tight-fitting Levis. His black hair gleamed with droplets of moisture. "Pretty much all of it. Don't worry, Merrill, I talk to the dogs all the time, too."

Merrill started to laugh. "They're comforting. I forget they're not human."

Buster licked her hand.

Jason grinned. "You mean they're not?"

"Thank you for keeping your sense of humor." She picked up Annie and nuzzled the dog.

"After my divorce from Serena being played out in front of what felt like the entire city of New York, I learned to keep my cool."

"One of the things taught in law school is to remain calm under pressure. But in the back of my head, I can't help wishing I had a gun."

"Merrill, I didn't think you were the type," he teased.

Merrill blushed. She hadn't thought so either. "Maybe an Uzi."

His eyes sparkled. "So you're a 'more bang for the buck' type of woman."

"I don't know if I'd put it that way, but you better believe it." She found herself tingling. The way he looked at her was so intimate, so familiar. The kind of look a man gave his lover.

The front door flung open, and J.D. and Belle Boyd tromped in.

Jason looked irritated. "The door bell works. This is not your house."

Belle Boyd glared at him. "By the time we're finished with you two, it will be."

Merrill took a deep breath. She was going to have to play referee again. "I don't recall issuing you an invitation to come over."

J.D. puffed out his chest. "We've had a thought."

"You're kidding," Jason said. "Merrill, get the newspaper on the phone. What's that reporter's name? The one who wrote that trashy story in this morning's paper."

Belle Boyd stomped her foot. "You have no cause to insult us in such a manner when we've come with a peace offering."

The puppy wriggled. Merrill set her down. The puppy ran up to Belle Boyd and J.D., sniffed briefly at their feet and suddenly squatted to let loose a gusher. A pool of puppy piddle spread around the soles of their shoes.

Belle Boyd screamed.

J.D. shrieked.

Merrill grabbed the puppy and whispered into her ear, "Good girl." Then she shook her finger in the puppy's face. "Bad puppy." Annie wriggled her fat little body and licked Merrill's chin.

Jason took the puppy. "Let's put the dogs outside."

"Where did you get that foul creature?" Belle Boyd looked as though she'd swallowed poison.

"She just showed up." Using the leftover pages of the newspaper she hadn't yet burned, Merrill mopped up the puddle.

"Another hungry mouth biting into my inheritance." J. D. paced the living room.

Merrill turned back to Belle Boyd and J.D. "What peace offering?"

J.D. straightened his tie. "Belle and I have discussed it. And we have decided that rather than filing a claim and going through all the complications of a hearing, we will settle out of court for fifty million dollars. We'll take the city property and the island, and we will not pursue our aunt's insanity."

Jason's eyebrows shot up. "Wait a minute, bud."

Merrill put a hand on his arm. "Jason, as Miss Eulalie and Psyche's legal counsel, I believe this is my territory." She studied Belle Boyd and her brother. Then she went up to J.D. and gently straightened the lapels on his jacket. "Why don't you fold your offer five ways, and shove it where the moon don't shine? Does that mean anything to you?"

J.D. stumbled back. Belle Boyd stepped forward and shook her gloved fist. "We gave you your chance, Merrill Prescott. Now, we're going to take everything. Every last dime. Every inch of property. You and that disreputable construction worker and those stupid dogs will be out on the street. Including the servants, because we're not going to leave them with one red dime."

"Go ahead," Merrill challenged.

J.D. stepped toward the door. "You'll never find anyone willing to testify on Miss Eulalie's behalf. Not after what was in the newspaper this morning."

Jason grabbed J.D. and slammed him against the wall. "Yo, Pretty Boy, if you keep messing 'wid' me, I'll make it so that the cops find you in the New Jersey River, the Hudson, the Mississippi and the Missouri."

J.D. went white. "Unhand me."

"Gladly." Jason pushed him toward the door. "Take your skirt, too."

J.D. looked confused. "My skirt?"

Jason pointed at Belle Boyd. "The broad."

Belle Boyd turned to Merrill. "How can you let that man abuse my brother in such a fashion? You're an officer of the court. You are bound to uphold the law."

Merrill shrugged. "I didn't see anything."

J.D. and Belle Boyd slammed out the front door. "We'll see you in court."

Merrill couldn't stop smiling. That had felt good. She knew she'd pay later, but right now she didn't care. She turned to Jason. "'Yo, Pretty Boy, if you keep messing wid me?' Where did that bit of dialogue come from?"

He gave her an innocent look. "I'm from New York."

She shook her head. "I don't think so."

He shrugged. "You got me dead to rights. I was watching a mobster flick last night. I've been dying to use that line. And this situation seemed the appropriate moment. Thanks for not ratting me out, Babe."

"Will you stop that."

He laughed. "Come on. Let's play frisbee with the dogs."

"What about the storm?"

"We'll take care of the house, then play with the dogs. We'll start with the upstairs. I have everything we need upstairs already."

They gathered up the supplies and went to separate rooms. All afternoon, the house rang with the sound of hammering. She ran up and down the ladder until she thought her legs would fall off. She handed Jason boards and kept his nail bucket full. Her back ached and her hands grew numb. By late afternoon, the wind had picked up. The air vibrated with tension. She didn't think the storm would bypass the city, but then, Charleston was a tough old town.

When the windows were boarded and the house snug from the storm, Jason put the ladder away while Merrill fixed them fresh lemonade to ease their thirst.

Jason entered the kitchen. He smelled of sawdust and sea breeze. He accepted the glass of lemonade and drank it down. She watched him. She wanted to touch him, to run her fingers along the ridge of arm muscles. She wanted to kiss him.

Merrill stepped back in surprise. Kiss him! She wanted more than a kiss. She found herself leaning back toward him, and suddenly he slid his arms around her and pulled her close.

Jason kissed her. His lips were warm and tender and lemony. Her hand drifted up his arm to his neck. He felt solid and alive.

His tongue probed her lips urgently. Her mouth opened. He moaned. She resonated with tension. She could think of nothing but him. Being in his arms was perfect. She pressed closer to him, wanting to feel his entire body against hers. A little voice inside her head told her to surrender to him. This was her chance to have everything she'd ever wanted.

She loved him, no matter how her grandmother would feel. She would love him forever. She wasn't sure how he felt about her. He made her feel free and alive, ready to take on the world, no matter the consequences.

Their kiss ended and she stared at him, her breath shallow with wanting for him.

"Merrill." His voice was husky.

She could feel her lips move, but no words came out.

He grinned at her. "I feel that way, too."

She nodded. "I'm not a rule breaker. You're my client, and I shouldn't be kissing you."

"You're fired." He grabbed her close, his hands entangling in her hair.

She giggled. "You can't fire me. Only Psyche can."

He laughed. "Then let's go ask her." He opened the kitchen door to the porch and whistled.

Neither Psyche nor Buster came running. Annie whined. She padded across the lawn and up the stairs, her long ears flapping. She rubbed against Merrill's leg, still whining.

Merrill picked the puppy up. "What's wrong?"

Annie licked her chin and moaned.

Jason absently patted the puppy and whistled for Buster and Psyche again. Neither dog showed up.

"We'd better look for them." Jason started down the stairs.

"Where would they go?" Merrill ran down to join him. "They never leave the property."

"I don't know."

Merrill started to worry. The wind grew stronger, rustling the branches. A streak of lightning lit the sky, and a few seconds later thunder rumbled through the heavens.

Jason went one way and Merrill the other. Something was wrong. Annie whined plaintively. She danced around Merrill's feet. Merrill searched through the bushes, calling to Buster and Psyche.

Jason shouted, "Over here."

Merrill raced around the house and to the edge of the privet hedges that separated the house from its neighbor.

Jason stood over Buster, who lay on the ground, unmoving. Jason knelt down gently examining his dog. "He's breathing, but he seems to be really asleep."

Merrill knelt next Buster. She patted the dog's head.

"I don't understand." Jason stroked the dog's rough fur.

"Where's Psyche?" Merrill pushed herself to her feet.

"She must be around somewhere."

Merrill left Jason to minister to his dog. She walked around the garage and the outlying cottages. No Psyche. How strange. She circled the garden, staring at the ground, not certain what she was looking for.

"Did you find Psycho?" Jason asked when she'd come full circle. He stood on the porch, Buster in his arms.

Merrill shook her head. "I have this really bad feeling."

"Me, too."

Jason put his dog in a sheltered corner of the porch and joined Merrill to search the grounds again.

"Look at that." Jason pointed to the ground.

Embedded in the flowers, Merrill saw a lavender high-heel from a woman's shoe. Belle Boyd had decked herself out in that color. Belle Boyd had been in the flower garden.

Merrill and Jason searched further. No Psyche.

Rain started. First a gentle, soothing rain, but within minutes a furious deluge blanketed the earth.

Merrill and Jason ran to the porch and stood under the shelter of the roof. Merrill held up the shoe heel. "I think she's been dog-napped. Belle Boyd and J.D. appear to have moved from extortion to kidnaping."

Jason examined the heel. "I don't believe it. Belle Boyd and J.D. couldn't find their way out of a paper bag, much less hatch a scheme like this."

"Don't kid yourself. Under all that taffeta and chiffon, Belle Boyd is a smart woman. And greed is a superb motivator. Besides, what other reason could there be for Psyche to be gone and for Buster to be so soundly asleep, like he's been drugged."

Jason stared at the shoe heel. "I think you watched the Scorsese film last night, too. She's hiding. Psycho hates storms, and even I can tell this one is going to be a humdinger."

Merrill grabbed his arm. "Listen to me. This yard is completely fenced in. The only way Psycho...I mean Psyche's Folly could get out is if someone took her out. I did a little criminal prosecution before I went into private practice. Belle and J.D. had motive, means and opportunity. They've kidnaped Psyche, and I expect they planned it." She watched as Jason's expression shifted. He believed her.

"What about a ransom note?" he asked.

"It'll come," Merrill said, "or we'll get a phone call."

"We need to call the police."

Merrill opened the kitchen door. "If we call the police right now, they'll simply say the dog is out wandering around and tell us to call animal control."

"We can't sit around doing nothing."

"If Belle Boyd and J.D. really are the dognappers, they aren't going to hurt Psyche. That dog is their meal ticket."

Jason shook his head. "I can't believe anyone would kidnap a dog." He held out the heel. "Or be so obvious about it."

Another streak of lightning lit the dark sky, followed by thunder so loud the house shook. Annie cowered against Merrill's legs. She picked up the puppy and cradled it in her arms. "I didn't say Belle Boyd was sensible. Just smarter than the average sea slug."

"What do you think we should do?"

Merrill glanced out the window at the rain drenching the garden. "We may have time to run over to Belle's house. That's the logical place to check first. J.D. has an apartment, and the landlord doesn't allow pets. I doubt he would want to draw attention to himself by taking the dog there."

Jason was halfway out the door. "Let's do it."

They drove quickly through the city. Rain battered the windshield. The sky grew darker and more threatening.

Belle Boyd lived in Mt. Pleasant. Her home was in a newer subdivision with wide, sweeping lawns and magnolia bushes forming the perimeter of the turn of the century structure. Green lawns stretched from the street to the front of the house.

Jason turned into the driveway and parked behind the house, which was dark. The rain came down harder. "Looks like no one's home."

Merrill pulled out an umbrella she found under the seat. "I'm surprised. I didn't think Belle Boyd was smart enough to go somewhere else."

"What do you want to do?"

"If I wasn't sworn to uphold the laws of the state, I'd say lets take a look inside."

"I'm not an officer of the court." He reached behind the back seat and grabbed his tool box. Then he walked to the back porch.

Merrill followed, the rain beating hard on the umbrella. "This is breaking and entering."

"I'm not breaking anything." He climbed the stairs leading to the wide, wrap-around porch. At the back door, he set his toolbox down and opened it, pulling out a black leather pouch.

Merrill leaned over his shoulder to see what he was doing. "What are those?" Long, narrow rods resided inside the pouch.

"Lock picks."

Merrill grabbed his arm. "You can't pick the lock. That's a felony in this state."

"Do you know how many of my customers forget to leave me a key?"

"You are not breaking into this house."

He punched the bell. Deep in the house, Merrill heard the chimes bang out the tune, Dixie. How corny! Belle Boyd liked to think she was the quintessential Southern belle, but in reality she was nothing more than a pampered, pretentious snob.

"See," Jason said. "No answer. We're going in."

"But, Jason, she could have an alarm system. Her husband could be taking a nap and not hear the chime."

Jason pushed a rod into the lock. "Belle's not paranoid enough for an alarm system, and her husband is probably wherever she is. We need to work fast. Psycho's life is at stake here."

Merrill grabbed his arm. "You're being overly dramatic. Belle Boyd is not going to hurt the dog."

He shrugged her off. "Guys aren't dramatic. Guys are heroic."

"That's good. Work on my guilt."

His fingers were dextrous as he gently probed the lock on the kitchen door. "I intended to."

She wondered how his fingers would feel on her skin. She blushed, feeling hot despite the cool air and the dampness of the coming storm.

"You're staring at me," Jason said.

"I'm sorry."

"Back off. You're making me nervous. It's been a long time since I broke the law."

"I know the details." The newspaper article was still fresh in her mind.

"I grew up in a rough neighborhood. What can I say?" He probed more deeply in the lock with his tools.

Merrill heard a click. In her mind, she imagined her mug shot with smeared makeup and messy hair. Her grandmother would be absolutely humiliated. Her parents had always asked for copies of their mug shots when they'd been arrested at their anti-something rallies. At least they would be proud of her. They'd add her picture to their own wall of fame on the inside of their Volkswagen van.

The door swung open and Jason glanced back at her in triumph. "Entrée."

Merrill mentally threw a pair of dice. They came up snake-eyes, so she was a loser either way. Merrill went inside. Belle Boyd's kitchen was large and airy and almost empty. No table, no chairs. Merrill peeked into several cupboards. No dishes. No anything.

The living room wall had faded areas on the wallpaper where Merrill suspected pictures had once hung. While Jason searched the house, Merrill gave in to her curiosity, hating herself even as she entered the downstairs study and opened the top drawer of the pressed wood desk. The desk, out of place with the opulent wallpaper, contained a stack of past due bills. Belle and her husband looked to be up to their eyeballs in debt. A quick glance through the stack, and a running total in her head, left Merrill gasping. She had thought her grandmother's situation to be dire, but Belle and her husband were on the fast track to bankruptcy court if they didn't see a large amount of cash soon.

On their own volition, Merrill's fingers opened the other drawers, and she found more bills. Even the power company was threatening to turn off their electricity.

Footsteps sounded in the hallway, and Jason entered the room.

"I found suitcases on the bed," he said, "like someone was packing to go somewhere."

"You looked through their closets?" she gasped.

He stared at her. "Excuse me, but it looks to me like your hand is in their desk drawer."

"I'm conducting an investigation. I am an officer of the court."

He grinned. "Because I swing a hammer, I'm snooping?"

Merrill nodded. "There is that fine line."

"Thank you for the legal clarification, Miss Merrill Prescott, Attorney at Law." He glanced around the room. "What did you find out about Belle Boyd Beaumont?"

"She's up to her crinolines in debt." Merrill pushed a few bills aside. She saw a receipt and frowned. "And here's the smoking gun."

"What are you talking about."

She held up the piece of paper by one corner, "This is a receipt from a vet for dog tranquilizers, dated yesterday."

"Let me see." He reached for the receipt.

"Careful. Just look. We don't want to leave any proof behind to show we were here. I've seen smart crooks squirm out of convictions because the police corrupted the crime scene. I'm erring on the side of caution."

He studied the receipt. "Explain a little bit more."

She dropped it back into the drawer. "Just by being here, we could screw up any investigation that may result from Belle Boyd's actions. Assuming she's the one who took Psyche." Covering the receipt with a stack of bills, she pulled the tail of her shirt out of the waistband and carefully closed the drawer. Then she wiped the front piece.

"What are you doing?"

"This never happened. We were never here. Get my drift."

"You have a devious mind."

"I'm a good attorney." She pointed at the door. "I want you to wipe every surface you touched. We have got to figure out some way for the police to get a search warrant. And if they do search the place, the last thing we want them to find out is we broke into this house."

"Assuming they believe us."

"We can't take chances. If they don't believe us, they don't. But if they do, we don't want any suspicion cast away from Belle and J.D."

"You have a crafty mind, lady."

She smiled primly. "Why, thank you."

"Any idea where they might go?"

Merrill shook her head. "Not a one."

"I think we should return to Eulalie's house and wait for the phone call or the note."

Merrill agreed. "I hate all this skullduggery."

"I don't."

Merrill pushed him out of the room and down the hall. "Clean up your mess and meet me in the truck. And don't touch anything else."

Merrill realized she had just had the most fun she'd had in a long time.

***

"I think the worst of the storm has finally arrived." Jason parked the truck in Eulalie's driveway. The trees around the courtyard whipped back and forth. Rain fell in torrents.

The wind buffeted the house. The timbers creaked and the structure shuddered with each new burst. In her bedroom, Merrill dialed Nana's number.

Blythe answered on the second ring. "Merrill, when are you coming over here?"

"Nana, I can't. We're having a situation."

"You know I hate waiting out a storm all by myself."

Merrill bit her lip. "I'll come get you, and bring you to Miss Eulalie's."

"No, you come here." Blythe's voice was sharp.

Merrill took a deep breath, trying to figure out how to explain about Psyche's Folly. "I can't. Psyche's Folly has been kidnapped."

"What would anyone want with a mangy old hound dog?"

"I can think of seventy-five million reasons," Merrill said more sharply than she intended.

Nana huffed. "Well then, you'd best stay where you are. Don't you worry about me. Carter is here, and he'll keep me company. He seems to want to spend hours and hours talking about nothing but you. I'm telling you, Merrill Prescott, this man is a catch. His stock portfolio is to die for."

Merrill leaned wearily against the wall. "Nana, you make him sound like some big, ole catfish."

"You are going to need someone to take care of you when I'm gone."

Like that was going to happen any time soon. Blythe was too ornery to die. "Nana, I take very good care of myself. I eat right, I get enough sleep and exercise. I have a career I love. I'm doing just fine without a man. Listen, I have to go. You take care."

"Don't forget," Blythe said, "you still need to pick out a gown for my cotillion."

"I won't forget. I'll call you tomorrow." Merrill disconnected before her grandmother could say more about the mythical man Merrill needed in her life. She didn't want a man. She wanted to pay off the family debts, take care of the darn dog, and get her own life in order before taking on another person's eccentricities.

***

Venus waved open a portal to J.D.'s cabin. Belle Boyd and J.D. sat at a kitchen table in J.D.'s hideaway on Lake Marian. Psyche was tied to a table leg and lay on the floor, looking miserable.

Cupid's heart went out to the animal. "Why did you have Belle and J.D. kidnap the dog?"

Venus patted his hand. "Everything will be fine, Cupie. I won't let anything happen to Psyche's Folly. I needed a little crisis to bring Merrill and Jason together. Especially since they didn't want us around. I still can't believe they fired us."

"Get over it, Mom. Back to the conversation." Keeping his mother focused seemed to be a full-time job. Come to think of it, one he wouldn't mind being fired from.

Venus giggled. "Belle Boyd and J.D. are so easy to manipulate, they seemed like the perfect answer. I couldn't pass up the opportunity. Now Jason and Merrill have something to work for."

"Are you sure Jupiter isn't going to be able to trace any of this back to us?"

Venus tilted her head at him. "Trust me."

"Didn't you say that to Guinevere and Lancelot?"

Venus shook her finger at him. "Listen, Merlin was a bitter old man. He got all bent out of shape because I broke up with him. So he sabotaged Lancie and Gwennie just to spite me. But that's okay. I fixed him good. He's not getting out of that tree for another millennia, if then."

Cupid hoped he never got on her bad side. He might be doing time in a rock or landfill.

Nine

Merrill walked downstairs as the electricity flickered. She was worried sick about Psyche, but had to hope Belle and J.D.'s greed would keep them from harming her.

Jason had spread a red-and-white checkered tablecloth on the floor in front of the fireplace. He'd turned on the gas, and a cheerful little flame flickered behind the glass doors.

"Better get the candles." Jason went into the kitchen.

Merrill sat down on the stool. Storms like this were old news for her. She didn't think this one would approach hurricane force. Still, she needed to be prepared. She wondered how Psyche was weathering the storm.

Just as Jason returned with the candles, the lights went out. Annie crawled into Merrill's lap, and Buster huddled against her knees.

Jason flipped on a butane lighter and lit the candles he'd placed on the fireplace mantle. "Well, my lady, you're going to have saltine crackers and peanut butter for dinner."

Merrill laughed. "I've had worse."

He lit more candles and arranged them on the tablecloth. The candles softened the hard lines and etched features of his face, making him look more mysterious and sensual.

Who was this man? What had brought him into her life? All of the men she'd dated in the past had treated her like a child. Even

Nana treated like her a child. Here she was, a college graduate, a successful attorney, and every time she was with Nana, Merrill still felt like she was five years old. Jason treated her like a grown woman. She liked that. With Jason, she could be herself. With him, she could be cranky, make stupid jokes, or use a hammer. And he didn't chide her for being unladylike.

Merrill studied him as he placed a jar of peanut butter on the floor and tore open a package of crackers. He lathered peanut butter onto one of the crackers and handed it to her. His hand brushed against hers, and she pulled away, her skin on fire.

Merrill had thought she had her life all planned out. And Jason Stavros hadn't been a part of it. Despite all her protestations to Nana only a few minutes ago, what she'd meant was that she didn't want a man her grandmother had chosen for her.

Just the sight of Jason on his knees sent her heart racing. She had never thought she would find a man she liked well enough to consider anything beyond a casual relationship. But Jason wasn't any man.

What would her grandmother think if Merrill confessed she had the hots for Jason? Blythe had her heart set on finding a rich husband for Merrill, so neither of them would have to worry about the future. Where she had failed with her son, Blythe intended to succeed with Merrill.

Merrill understood where Nana was coming from. The loss of the family money had been a blow of such magnitude Nana had been in denial ever since. Out of love, Merrill tried to keep up appearances so her grandmother wouldn't suffer public embarrassment, but she had done so at the expense of her own future. She hadn't wanted to be an estate lawyer. Her first job had been with the District Attorney's office because she'd wanted to be one of the good guys. Unfortunately, there had been no money in preserving the justice system. Repairing the family fortunes and caring for Blythe had come first.

"Merrill, where are you?" Jason waved his hand in front of her face.

Merrill sighed. "Thinking. My life has taken such a detour."

"Hasn't everybody's?"

She munched her cracker and brushed the crumbs off her lap. Annie licked up the crumbs, her stubby tail wagging furiously. "Not the Prescotts, or so Nana would have the world believe."

"Interesting old lady, your grandmother."

Merrill accepted another cracker from him. "Actually, she's quite easy to understand. Money, marriage and grandchildren. In that order."

Jason chuckled. "Has she always been this obsessed with money?"

"Always." Merrill chewed. She wondered if Nana knew what it was like to be swept away by love. Merrill's stomach clenched. Everything about Jason was so wonderful. She wanted to run her hands down his body, touching every inch. She didn't think she'd ever be satisfied until she knew every muscle, every part of him.

Annie stuck her head in Merrill's lap and licked up more of the crumbs. Merrill pushed her off her lap. "Money is important. Nana came from a long line of wealthy people. My grandfather came from a long line of wealthy people. Wealth is intermingled with her self-esteem."

"That's a lot of weight for you to carry. What about your parents?" He lay on the floor, leaning on his elbow. His eyes reflected the flickering light from the candles. He looked like he understood every word she said and sympathized.

"My dad was lucky." She'd never spoken to anyone about her past, but Jason made her feel comfortable enough to do so. "None of those things that Nana held dear mattered to him. He met my mother, and it was love at first sight. The kind of love that rearranged his entire life. Their first date was at a civil rights demonstration." Her parents had the kind of love Merrill wanted. Everlasting. Consuming. Real.

Jason ate a cracker. "Your parents sound interesting."

"They are."

"You sound like you miss them."

"Every day, but the gypsy lifestyle isn't for me. I like structure. Nana offered me security."

Jason sat up and scooted over to sit near her. He ran a finger along her cheek. The skin of his finger was rough but pleasurable.

She leaned close to him, breathing in his scent, feeling his strength. She realized that she'd changed from the woman who had first entered this house. Love had changed her. Her love for him gave her confidence. A week ago she would never have allowed herself to be drawn into a relationship with a man like Jason. She would have considered Nana's feelings first and her own second. Even though she could never have a real affair with him because of the ethics of her profession, she would never deny herself again. She would live her life for herself, and by her own rules. She would never go back to the Merrill Prescott who danced to her grandmother's tune.

He touched the base of her neck. She nestled against him. "Jason," she moaned, "we have to stop."

"I want you."

"You can't want me." Her words sounded false. She wanted him, even though she had to deny herself. She had wanted him since he'd walked into her office, all dirty and greasy.

Jason's hand slid to her breast. "We've been dancing around the issue since you moved in here."

"I know."

He nodded smiling. "Go on." His voice held a teasing quality.

"I'm attracted to you, but any kind of relationship would be completely inappropriate." There, she'd said it. "We've already discussed this."

"I don't believe you. I don't even think *you* believe you."

Merrill shuddered. He was right. No matter how wrong her feelings for him were, she couldn't give in. "Psyche is my client." Her voice held a desperate tone.

Jason shrugged. "She's a dog."

Merrill held up her hands, trying to think up another good reason. "I'm still her attorney."

Jason laughed. The candlelight illuminated the darkness of his eyes, highlighting the desire shining in their depths.

"What's so funny?" Merrill asked.

"This is the first time you've talked about being Psycho's attorney without a bit of contempt in your voice."

"This case is so strange. I think I'm the only dog lawyer in the free world."

"Yet, you fight tooth and nail for Eulalie."

"Miss Eulalie was not crazy. And it's my job to make sure everyone in Charleston knows that, too."

His kissed her. Without thought, she responded.

"If you're Psycho's attorney, and I'm custodian, does that make you my attorney, too?"

"Of course."

"Then I have a last wish."

She knew what he was going to say. She waited, holding her breath. He slid his arms around her and nuzzled her neck.

"Make love with me." He leaned forward and kissed her. "It's my last wish."

Ethics be damned. How could she deny him? She wanted him, too.

Merrill moaned as his tongue gently stroked her lips and slipped into her mouth. She touched his cheek. Stubble scraped the palm of her hand.

Jason pushed her back until she was flush on the floor.

Merrill couldn't believe this. Here she was about to make love to the most beautiful man she had ever seen. She never got this lucky in love.

She arched her back to get closer to him just to prove this was real and not a figment of her lonely, love-starved imagination.

Jason began to unbutton her blouse. The tips of his fingers grazed her skin. Merrill slid her hands down his side, pulling him closer.

Jason whispered, "Tell me you want me."

Merrill moved under him, letting his weight sink onto her. She felt his excitement pressed into the juncture of her thighs. "I do ... more than anything."

"Good." The tip of his tongue ran along the valley of her breasts.

Tingling sensations ran up and down her spine as she fought to breathe. Merrill hadn't ever felt so free and light-headed. Jason was responsible for her new feelings of freedom.

He unsnapped the front hook of her bra and pushed the lacy cup aside. For a second he just stared down at her. "You're perfect." He touched her hardened nipple with the tip of his tongue.

Heat and desire rushed through her. She arched her back, inviting him to take her into his mouth. His mouth descended on her skin. Merrill sucked in a quick breath. She bit her lip to stop from crying out from the dazzling sensations pulsing through her. His tongue and mouth worked the most glorious magic on her body and soul. She forgot her fears and trepidation. This was perfect, like making love was supposed to be. As his lips nuzzled her throat Merrill, sank her fingers into his thick hair.

Suddenly he was off her and pulling her to her feet. She didn't think she could stand. She leaned, clutching at him. He swung her up into his arms and carried her from the library and up the stairs.

Sheltered in his strong arms, she felt his heart beating next to hers. "Where are we going?"

"Someplace where we can be alone."

Merrill looked back and noticed the dogs following them. She giggled. "I forgot about our audience."

"Stay Buster. Daddy can do this one alone."

She laughed. "You're so silly."

He stopped at the door to her bedroom. "Didn't anyone tell you not to talk about a man's sense of humor at this critical juncture?"

"No."

Buster barked. Annie started to whine.

"Poor things. They think we don't love them anymore."

"I can accept that."

With her tucked tight against his chest, Jason managed to open the door. He was nervous. Merrill was so warm and willing in his arms, he didn't know if he could make it to the actual lovemaking part. What a time for him to suffer an anxiety attack. He used to be really good at sex. The last time he was this nervous he was sixteen-years-old in the back of his dad's Chevy Impala with Marlena Costas.

He set Merrill on the bed. She looked at him with such heat in her eyes, he thought he would fall over. For all those cool, classic airs Merrill showed to the rest of the world, she knew how to burn. "Are you nervous?"

"No."

He tried to calm his racing heart. "Good, I'm glad one of us isn't."

She stuck the tip of her tongue out and licked her lips.

The heat circulating through him kicked up a notch. Her mouth looked ripe, swollen from his kisses. He sat on the bed, trying to remember his own name. How did he get this lucky?

She lifted his hand and guided it to her bared breast. She covered the back of his hand with both of hers. Merrill looked at him with such trust and desire, he felt humbled. The softness of her breast filled his hand. He couldn't talk. Couldn't think. All he wanted was Merrill.

"Make love to me, Jason. Now."

Quickly they shed their clothes. Jason pressed her down until she was flat on the mattress. Her soft skin warmed him. He couldn't feel anything except her. She smelled of peaches ripening in the summer heat. With her breasts crushed against his chest, she moaned.

For a few minutes he wanted to just kiss her and stroke her. Even as his body demanded he take her and satisfy his escalating lust, he hesitated, wanting her to be ready for him. Merrill needed time and patience. He wanted her to have as much pleasure as he knew he would have.

Merrill wrapped her legs around his hips. Jason slipped his hand between their bodies and began to stroke her. Her wetness surrounded his finger as her muscles contracted around him. "Tell me what you want. Tell me what you like."

"I like this." She shuddered, digging her heels into his hips. "I like all the things you've done so far."

"Good, I intend to do more."

"Like what?"

Jason slipped his finger deeper inside her. She clamped around him, holding him inside. Merrill moaned. A low moan that contained all the passion, all the desire she had for him. Her eyes darkened to a stormy blue as though she kept pace with the storm raging outside. Jason pressed deep into her and rocked. He kissed her lips, tasting her sweetness, then slid another finger inside her. Merrill bit his lip as he probed. "Merrill—"

"Now, Jason. Now."

Jason lifted himself off her. He intended to get his pants and hopefully find a condom, but Merrill slid her leg over his, and he had to taste her one more time. He started with her breasts, working his mouth over her nipples and the underside of her delicate skin. With the tip of his tongue, he journeyed down to her flat stomach and plunged into her navel. She went stiff on him. She grabbed his hair in both her hands and held his head down. He could hear her breathy words of encouragement to go further. He was game. He slid down to the apex of her thighs, nipping and sucking every inch of her damp skin.

She twisted under him, begging and pleading for him to stop. He gripped her squirming hips, holding her still. Shifting, he eased his tongue inside her, plunging deep over and over again, tasting her, licking the nub of her core. Spasms began to work through her body, and Jason continued until she cried out. When her climax ended, he kissed her breasts, moving upward to her mouth once more.

Merrill kissed him. "I want more."

Jason smiled. She was going to get the best he had to give. He reached for his pants and found the lone condom his dad had given him on the day his divorce was final. Quickly he sheathed himself.

Merrill sat up and planted her hands on his shoulders and pushed him down to the mattress. "You're taking too long." She straddled him and eased down his shaft until he was completely submerged inside her. Slowly, she rocked back and forth.

Jason gripped her hips, guiding her.

She kissed him, plunging her tongue into his mouth, her hair tickling his chest. She was slick and wet with desire. She kept up a furious pace until he thought he would explode. Then her body began to shudder into explosive spasms that rocked them both.

Merrill increased her tempo, grinding her sex against him. Her internal muscles stiffened around him. She trembled as she erupted into climax. Fire surrounded him, and Jason let go. Waves of pleasure washed over him. His body shook. For a long moment he was suspended in a web of ecstasy that seemed to go forever. He felt immortal, and his power gave him strength.

Merrill collapsed against him. Her skin was dewy from lovemaking. Jason pulled her closer.

He loved her. He had no idea how or why his feelings for her had grown so strong. He'd had no intention of ever falling in love again, and while he wasn't looking, she'd burrowed into his heart and soul. He was half frightened and half exhilarated. Frightened because he'd already experienced the worst love had to offer. And exhilarated because he sensed Merrill would be the very best he'd ever known.

***

A roar of thunder woke Jason. For a minute he didn't know where he was. He lay in a warm bed, snuggled up against a warm body. A warm body! Something fuzzy tickled his nose. He sniffed. It was Merrill's hair. He would recognize that unique smell anywhere. Heat rushed to his belly. Merrill Prescott. All the memories of the evening before rushed back to him.

He stroked the tendril of her hair, brushing it against his cheek. Her hair was silken soft and clean-smelling. Serena had always smelled of designer perfume, even in bed. He never knew what she smelled like underneath. Merrill smelled clean. He liked that.

He gently stroked her body, his fingers lingering on her breasts. She moaned in her sleep and turned, her hands reaching for him. When she snuggled tight against him, a great welling of tenderness surprised him. He didn't think he'd had that feeling in him any more. He'd thought Serena had ripped all the sentiment from him.

Buster whined, pushing a cold nose into his thigh. He knew what that whine meant, and if Buster needed to go out, then so did Annie. He needed to put in a doggie door so the animals could let themselves in and out.

Remembering Buster also brought worry of Psycho back to his mind. Was she all right? Eulalie had loved that dog like a child. He felt a moment of irritation at Belle and J.D. for taking the dog. Buster whined again, and Annie gave a short yip.

Easing out of bed, Jason reached for his jeans. His foot collided with fur. Buster licked his knee. The sight of Merrill curled on her side, her hair spread about the pillow, left him gasping. He wanted nothing more than to crawl back in with her and wake that luscious mouth with kisses.

He needed to think. He knew Merrill was wary of him. He didn't want to crowd or push her. He realized that she'd taken a big step. Everything that Eulalie had said about Blythe Prescott had led him to believe that Merrill was having trouble severing the apron strings. In going to bed with him, Merrill had shown a streak of rebellion similar to what her own father had done. He liked that. He'd always wanted a rebellious woman who kept life interesting and the sex hot. Merrill was hot. Beneath her ice queen facade, she burned like melted lava.

In his own room, he changed to jogging clothes while Buster and Annie waited patiently. He unlatched the storm shutters and peered outside. Dawn was just lighting the sky. Streaks of orange and yellow pierced the darkness. The blinking of his clock radio told him the electricity was back on.

He loved the early morning best, when the city was still asleep, and the air was clean and sharp. While the dogs did their business, he ran on the deserted streets, the sound of the ocean a distant roar. The receding storm was a black cloud to the north. Salt air stung his face. The sidewalks were wet.

He could lose himself in the run. Before his divorce, he'd been training for the New York Marathon, but afterward, the race no longer mattered. He'd wanted nothing more than to get as far away from New York and Serena as he could.

As he jogged, he thought about Psycho and where Belle Boyd might keep the dog. He thought about Merrill. She'd turned out to be a sweet, compassionate, forthright woman. He had fallen in love with her. Despite their night of passion, he didn't believe she'd ever love him back. And even if she did, Merrill still deserved a man who had the same background as she did. Someone who was gentle and cultured. She didn't need a rough and tumble person like him who didn't know a salad fork from a desert spoon.

How was he going to get through the next years being so close to her, yet unable to touch her heart? Last night, she'd shown him that a special chemistry existed between them. Their lovemaking had been wild and passionate, yet sweet and touching.

He ran harder. He scanned the empty streets, the thought of finding Psycho always in the back of his mind. They should call the police, but her point about the police not believing them had been well taken. And with the cleanup after the storm, the police would be busy with other things. They'd have no interest in a lost dog. Even a dog worth seventy-five million dollars.

How careless of them to lose the dog. He wondered if there was any contingency in the will to replace them if they should prove unfit parents.

He and Merrill would have to find Psycho. The fact that they had received no note or phone call made him wonder if Belle Boyd and J.D. really were the culprits. Maybe Psycho had just wandered away. But that didn't explain why Buster was drugged, and how Belle's shoe heel had come to break off in the garden.

He pulled gulps of air into his lungs as he turned down the last stretch of his run. The sun had pierced the clouds and brought brightness and light to the city. Steam rose from the ground. It would be a hot day.

He turned into the driveway and slid to a halt. In the center of the driveway stood a police officer, his car parked near the garage. He bent over a box on the path leading to the kitchen door.

The police officer straightened. "Morning. I'm Officer John Barnett. Are you the dog guy?"

Jason nodded. He approached cautiously, wondering if Merrill had called the cops after all to report the kidnaping.

Officer Barnett gestured at the box. "I didn't know what to do with them."

Jason peered into the box. Five whimpering puppies huddled together, drenched and cold. One of the puppies stretched out on its side, eyes closed, looking dead.

Barnett gently stroked a puppy. "I found them in a drainage ditch near their mother's body. The shelter is stuffed with strays, and I thought of you."

Jason found himself grinning. "What's another five mouths to feed."

"Do you really work for the dog that inherited the seventy-five million dollars?"

"Yep." Jason reached for the box.

"How does a dog sign your paycheck?"

"With her paws."

Barnett looked startled, then started to grin. "Have you ever tried to forge the signature?"

"I'm working on it." Jason patted one of the puppies. The animal tried to suckle on his finger. "Speaking of our seventy-five million dollar mutt, we have a little problem here. I want to file a missing dog report."

"You lost your seventy-five million dollar dog?"

"The dog had a little help. Want some coffee before you head back?" Jason felt silly filing a dognapping report. Was dognapping even a crime?

"You mean your dog was stolen? I want to hear this story. I'll take that cup of coffee." The officer followed Jason into the house.

Merrill stood at the stove looking rumpled and infinitely desirable in her robe and fluffy slippers, her hair cascading down her shoulders. Jason sniffed. Wonderful smells emanated from the stove. He'd always wanted a woman who could cook.

Merrill eyed the cop. "Officer, you look tired. Would you like some coffee?"

She poured him a mug, and he cradled it in his hands.

Jason handed her the box. She glanced inside. "Oh, dear. They're ice cold." She opened a drawer, pulled out a stack of kitchen towels and started rubbing them dry. "I saw a heating pad in the pantry. Jason, get it, and we'll put the box on it."

While Jason plugged in the heating pad, Merrill vigorously rubbed the five puppies dry. Jason brought a bowl of puppy kibble. They ate and immediately went to sleep all tumbled together as only puppies could.

Merrill gently padded the side of the box with towels. "This house is beginning to resemble a Disney film."

Barnett chuckled. He accepted a mug of coffee and sat at the kitchen table, a spiral notebook opened in front of him. "So tell me about your missing dog."

"You told him," Merrill said to Jason.

He nodded. "I had to. It's for the best."

While the cop wrote, Merrill and Jason related an edited version of the facts, without telling about breaking into Belle's house and finding the vet bill.

After Barnett left, Merrill watched Jason. She felt awkward. After a night of such intense passion, she didn't know what to feel about him. "About last night."

"Great, wasn't it." He looked eager and happy.

She blushed. Ecstasy was closer to her definition. She couldn't love him. Not yet. Not now. She frowned.

He reached out to take her hand. His touch sent electrical tingles through her body. "Tell me what's wrong, Merrill."

"I'm really confused about last night."

"What's to be confused about? We were perfect together."

"That's the problem."

He stared at her. "I don't understand."

"I don't either." Miserable, she withdrew her hand. How could she explain to him that she didn't think she could handle being in love with him. They would be together for a long time. Did she want to take that risk? What would happen when they fell out of love, but they were still together because of Psyche?

Merrill couldn't afford to skip out of her obligations—financially or morally. She needed the money the executorship would bring her. That money would go a long way toward settling the family debts.

"Merrill, I love you."

"No, you can't. The timing is off."

He shook his head. "Timing? What does that have to do with love?"

"You don't understand."

"Then make me understand."

Helpless, Merrill could only stare at him. Frustrated, she didn't know how she could explain what was going on in her head. "I'm being pulled in too many directions right now. I need time to think."

She ran out of the kitchen, afraid that if she stayed she'd throw caution to the wind and allow herself to act on her feelings without any worry about the ramifications.

***

Venus was so glad Belle had the foresight to have a full-length mirror in the cabin. Venus paraded in front of the mirror admiring the way Psyche's ears flopped over and the intricate curl of her fleecy fur. Psyche was gorgeous, and Venus loved being in her skin, or should she say fur.

"That dog is doing it again," J.D. said.

"Doing what?" Belle painted her fingernails.

"Admiring herself in the mirror."

Belle smiled. "She knows beauty when she sees it."

Venus would have grinned, but the dog's lips didn't work that way. At least Belle understood how devastatingly cute Psyche was. Venus admired her tail. She even had a cute butt.

"Should we call now?" J.D. asked.

Belle sat on a scruffy sofa admiring her nails. "Not yet. We need to give them more time."

J.D. paced back and forth. "We've given them twenty-four hours."

"Sit down or go take a nap with Henry in the other room. You make me nervous. You have to start thinking like a criminal. The longer we wait, the more they sweat and worry. And the more they worry, the more likely they are to part with all our lovely money."

Venus barked. Here she was, the most gorgeous dog ever to walk the earth, and all they could think about was money. Money was the worst thing her father had ever invented.

J.D. plopped down onto a chair. "I can't believe I've been reduced to dognapping."

"These are desperate times. We need to take desperate measures to get what is rightfully ours."

Venus felt a tug on her ear. Cupid, the size of a fly, buzzed about her eyes and then landed on her nose.

"Hey, Ma. I have news," he squeaked.

Venus nodded. She shook the dog body and released herself from Psyche's mind. "You be careful, honey. I'll be back. You sit quiet and don't let Belle scare you."

The dog whined. Venus floated up to the rafters with Cupid as he winked back to his regular shape. They sat on the log and watched Belle and J.D.

"Did Merrill and Jason...you know?" She nudged her son.

"About four times."

Venus gave her son a high-five, but she missed Cupid's hand and slapped him in the head. "Sorry, Cupie. I'm still working on that."

"It's a simple hand gesture, Ma."

Venus shrugged. "You know I'm not too coordinated. Besides, I don't want to mess up my manicure."

"Fine. Is the dog all right? They haven't hurt her, have they?"

Venus smiled at Psyche who watched them from the floor. "She's fine. Psyche understands that we're on a covert mission. She understands about Merrill and Jason, and approves."

"You've been discussing strategy with the dog."

"She's very smart, and pretty." She blew Psyche a phantom kiss. The dog wagged her tail and jumped up and down playfully.

J.D. started to kick her, but Belle stopped him.

Cupid snapped his fingers and froze them in place. "When this is over, I am going to roast him in the Underworld for all eternity."

Venus patted his shoulder. "Don't worry, Cupie, the Furies will hound them until the last of their days." She giggled. "Pardon my pun."

Cupid rolled his eyes. "I want to hurt them now."

"After our mission is completed."

Cupid gave her a strange look. "Mission. Strategy. Have you been reading spy thrillers again?"

"I have to keep my skills up."

"You miss the spy biz, don't you?"

Venus sighed. "Life hasn't been much fun since the Cold War ended."

"Calm down, Mom. What are we going to do about them?" He pointed at J.D. and Belle Boyd.

Venus tilted her head to study them. "I told you if the dog disappeared, Merrill and Jason would get closer and 'do the deed'. Now all we have to do is prevent Daddy from screwing things up. Can you believe he thought his old bag of tricks would work? My diamond bracelet and my fur coat. Like they would work unless I wanted them to. Daddy doesn't realize that modern women just aren't that easily impressed. If the man was smart, he'd have given her stock options or a mutual fund."

"What do you think he's going to try next?"

Venus tilted her head, thinking. "I don't know. Maybe the old come-to-her-as-a-swan trick or a puff of smoke. He's just never been very creative. I gave him his best ideas and, of course, now he can't come to me because we're not allowed to mess with the mortals anymore. He always did have a knack for painting himself into a corner."

"How are we going to stop him?"

Venus drummed her fingers on the rafter, thinking. A little twinge came into her head. Her hair started to hurt. "In the old days, creating a scandal used to be so much easier. Nowadays, there are no taboos. Unless we do something really bad, he'll end up on the Jerry Springer Show, making millions."

"You're stalling for time, aren't you?"

Venus shrugged. "It's that apparent, huh?" She hated when Cupie could see through her.

"I thought you had an idea for a scandal."

"I thought about some money scandal, but you know what they say about mortal justice. The more money you steal, the less time you do. And then you end up as a financial advisor on the national news."

"Does it have to be money?" Cupid frowned at J.D. and Belle, frozen in place looking like mannequins. "Maybe we should keep them frozen until we need them again?"

"No." Venus said. "We need to use them."

Cupid tapped his forehead. "I have it."

"What?" Venus turned to him eagerly. Cupid came up with terrific ideas.

"We could give Gramps a wife."

Venus whirled and snapped her fingers. "No. We could give him *three* wives."

"That's illegal."

"Exactly." Venus shook herself with delight. "When I'm done with Daddy, he'll never interfere in my job again."

She snapped her fingers once more. J.D. and Belle popped back to life. "Come on, Cupie. Let's get us some volunteers." And she disappeared in a puff of smoke.

TEN

Merrill sat in the kitchen with two of the puppies on her lap. They wriggled ecstatically as she tickled their tummies. She'd gone from having no pets to eight dogs in the space of a few days.

Annie leaped back and forth, playing with her ball, and Buster napped in a patch of sun. Through the open window, Merrill watched Jason as he replaced a board ripped off one of the cottages during the storm.

Jason looked good with the sunlight on his hair and his bare chest dewy with perspiration. She caught her breath. She'd just spent the night with this man, and he'd transported her to new heights.

She'd never lost her mind over a man's body before. He was so incredibly beautiful with his rippling muscles and tanned skin. She liked a man who vibrated with dark, smoldering sensuality. She wanted a man with calluses on his hand. She wanted Jason.

Every fiber of her being screamed out to him. Something had happened to her during the night. Something wild and wonderful. She wanted to talk to him, but she had so much to do. If the house hadn't taken such a beating in the storm, he would have accompanied her to the animal shelters. The police officer had suggested it, just to make sure Psyche hadn't accidentally run off.

She hadn't been able to make a decision about her relationship with Jason. She wanted him, and she knew she loved him. But how would she walk the fine line between lover and client?

The phone rang, preventing her from answering her question. "Hello."

A muffled voice answered. "We have the dog."

Merrill sat up straight. "J.D., is that you?"

"Did you read the letter?"

"What letter?" Merrill looked around the kitchen.

"The one in the mailbox." His voice rose in frustration.

"You're kidding me." Merrill had to restrain her laughter.

"Where else would someone put a letter?"

"We haven't read the letter." Merrill opened the door. With the palm of her hand covering the mouthpiece, she yelled for Jason. He stopped hammering and looked up. She waved him into the house. "What do you want, J.D.?"

"We want fifty million in cash. Small, unmarked bills."

"J.D.," Merrill said, "just bring Psyche back and we'll forget the whole thing."

"I'll hurt the dog." J.D. sounded desperate.

"No, you won't."

A long pause ensued. Jason ran to the door, and Merrill covered the mouthpiece. "Go look in the mailbox. Hurry. I have J.D. on the phone."

"Fifty million," J.D. repeated. "Tomorrow night. St. Michael's. Five o'clock. If you're late, I'll cut off one of the dog's ears."

"Tomorrow night! J.D., my grandmother's cotillion is tomorrow night. Not only can I not come up with that amount of cash in such a short time, I'm not going to deliver all that money wearing a designer ball gown and high heels."

"I'm not J.D."

"Yes, you are."

"I'm not."

"I'm not stupid, J.D."

Jason returned, holding a soggy envelope. He carefully opened it and drew out a sheet of paper with lettering cut from magazines.

He held it out to Merrill who read, *We have the dog. We'll phone you—soon.* "J.D.," Merrill warned, "don't you harm that dog. If you do, I swear to God I'll break your legs."

"I'm not J.D." He hung up.

Jason folded up the note. "J.D. called, I see."

"I can't believe it! The man actually had the gall to ask for fifty million."

Jason whistled. "That's a lot of dog biscuits."

"He wants the money tomorrow night."

"How does he think we're going to put that together in twenty-four hours?"

"I don't know. As though I don't have enough to do." She tapped herself on the forehead. "Oh my. I forgot!"

"Forgot what?"

"I don't have an escort for tomorrow night." The last person she wanted to ask was Carter Shelby-Rutledge. If she did, she'd never get rid of him, and he'd think she owed him.

"The dog is kidnapped, and you're worried about your escort for tomorrow tonight?"

"I don't have one." She rubbed her temples. "Jason, I know in the scheme of things this cotillion doesn't even register a blip on the scale, but you don't know my grandmother. If Blythe is not happy, then the whole city of Charleston is not happy. As she so frequently reminds me, she does not have much time left on this Earth, so I like to make her happy. I need an escort." She paused, took a deep breath and smiled. "Are you free tomorrow night, and do you have a tuxedo?"

"My tux is an Armani."

Merrill stared at him. She took a deep breath to still her pulse. Just the image of him filling out every sleek inch of an Armani tuxedo made her giddy.

He touched her on the cheek. "The cotillion is settled. Let's get back to the dog."

She shook herself. "Right." She forced her mind away from him in a tux and back to Psyche. "That blithering idiot J.D. wants the cash in small bills, delivered to St. Michael's Episcopal tomorrow night at five. I was christened at St. Michael's." Her voice rose. "I attend St. Michael's church almost every Sunday. Can you imagine the horror? There has to be a Commandment for desecrating the front steps of a church with extortion money. And," her voice went a note higher, "do you realize how many suitcases we would need for fifty million dollars? Does J.D. think I'll just run over to the bank with my trusty ATM card and make a withdrawal?"

Jason started laughing. He leaned against the door jamb and held his arms across his stomach and continued to laugh until he had to sit down.

Merrill put her hands on her hips and glared. "This is not funny. I have come up against some pretty stupid criminals in my days in the D.A.'s office, but J.D. and Belle take the cake. In fact, they take the whole bakery."

Between gusts of laughter, Jason said, "You sound more annoyed than anything else."

"I can just see myself tottering up the steps in high heels, lugging five hundred suitcases full of twenty dollar bills."

"I think this is a job for the cops." Jason picked up Officer Barnett's business card. "Why don't we just call him and let him handle it?"

**

Jupiter checked his book of spells. He needed a sure-fire love charm. Too bad he couldn't ask Venus. She would know what to do. As soon as he seduced Merrill, he was ending this hands-off human policy. What had he been thinking?

He flipped through the book. Swan? No. Puff of smoke? Been there, done that. He couldn't believe Merrill was resisting him. He had the sophisticated *savois-faire* of Cary Grant. The blonde Nordic looks of a young Kevin Costner. All he needed now was the beautiful Merrill Prescott to adorn his arm.

Snake? No. Mouse? No. Puppy? He stared at puppy for a moment. Lost dogs? A possibility. Merrill did like animals. He could turn her into an animal. That had worked once with that cute little water sprite. Who knew he could have so much fun as a sea otter? No. That wasn't as much fun as mortal to mortal. And Merrill wasn't like a water sprite, easily changed and easily returned.

He thought about the night he'd played cards with Mars, Vulcan and Pluto. Mars had mentioned he'd once turned himself into the husband of a very sexy French baroness during the Napoleonic Wars. Jupiter thought about Jason Stavros. He was a good looking man. Jupiter could do worse. If the love spells didn't work, then he could just turn himself into Jason and have a good time. He liked that idea and congratulated himself on his ingenuity.

He knew how this affair should go. Why wasn't she playing by the rules? If he didn't think anyone would catch him, he'd get rid of the construction worker with a snap of his fingers and have Merrill at his leisure. He was a god who needed many amusements to keep him interested.

"Why are you all dressed up, Daddy?" Venus called.

Jupiter whirled around. "Venus." He kissed her on the cheek. "Your sisters, the Camenae, are...uh...having a costume party. Yeah! That's right. One of their art benefits, and I'm going as a mortal."

Her critical gaze swept him up and down. "You look very nice indeed, Daddy."

"Thank you, Pumpkin. What are you doing tonight?"

She sighed. "Nothing."

"Don't tell me you and Mars are still feuding."

She nodded. "He and the Fruit Tree Floozy are pollinating fruit trees. Can you believe it?"

Jupiter touched her shoulder. "Honey, if you gave in to Mars once in a while, maybe he'd be with you and not her."

"Daddy, are you giving me romance advice?" Her eyebrows rose. "I thought I was the Goddess of Love. Oops!" She shook her head. "I forgot. I'm not allowed to practice anymore."

"Venus, don't you think things are working out just fine without our guidance?"

"No. In the last week, I've had seven pedicures and a massage every day. I lie around on a chaise like a lump on a log, watching TV. Frankly, Daddy, I'm bored." She pouted at him.

Jupiter needed to pacify her. When his darling daughter got bored, she got into trouble, and who knew what havoc she'd wreak on the gods. "I've been thinking. Even though I like my new policy, maybe in a month or two, I'll review it. And if things are no better or no worse then when we had a hand in things, I'll make changes."

She jumped up and down like a child. "Really, Daddy. You'd do that? For little ole me?"

Jupiter frowned. Where did she get that accent? Where had he heard that voice before? He hated when things eluded him. "Of course, sweetheart. Your happiness is very important to me. You are my favorite." He glanced at the hourglass. "Sorry, Pumpkin, hate to be late for your sisters' party."

"How come I didn't get an invite?" She tilted her head to look at him.

He patted her head. "You know how things are between half-sisters."

She wriggled her fingers at him. "You say hello for me." She disappeared with a snap of her fingers.

Jupiter heaved a huge sigh of relief and mopped his forehead. He was sweating! He hadn't sweated like this since the Titans challenged his authority, and he banished them for all eternity into the Abyss.

He pushed the thoughts away. He had a woman to seduce and couldn't be bothered by anything else. He opened a portal to the mortal world and stepped through it, his heart racing at the thought of Merrill Prescott. He was going to have her tonight.

***

"Okay," Venus said to the Furies. She surveyed them with a critical eye. "You're going down there masquerading as his wives and blow his gig."

The three Furies hissed or giggled. Venus was never sure with them. Their snake heads bobbed up and down.

"Now, did everybody rehearse their lines?"

They nodded in agreement and gave a thumbs up sign.

Venus grinned. "Don't forget your names now."

They all nodded again. One by one they transformed, shedding their snake skin to look like mortal women.

Venus could hardly contain herself. "You are all so pretty." She patted her hair. "But not as pretty as I am. Okay, girls, let's go."

Venus waved her hand above her head. A tornado formed and took them all down to Earth.

***

Merrill stood in front of the floor-to-ceiling mirror, staring at her image. She didn't recognize herself. The ice-blue ball gown flared out over her hips. Merrill adjusted the strapless bodice. She couldn't believe how she was about to con J.D. and Belle Boyd. She felt a thrill to know she had a streak of her grandmother's vindictiveness in her after all. Her peace-loving parents would be so horrified to know they hadn't stamped it out.

A knock sounded. Jason opened the door and walked into her room, whistling at the sight of her. "Wow!"

Merrill's cheeks grew hot. She hadn't had a compliment so sincere in more years than she wanted to count. "Thank you." She felt breathless.

The Armani tuxedo fit exactly the way she'd imagined. This was what a real man was supposed to look like in a black tuxedo—sophisticated and dashing, with just a hint of wickedness. She grew faint with the heat of desire spreading through her. Every nerve ending tingled. Their one night of passion had haunted her with such intensity she could barely breathe. "Wow, yourself."

"Thanks." He stepped into the room, one hand hidden behind his back. "You're beautiful."

She could see the truth of his words in his eyes.

"I brought you something." He held out a long, narrow velvet-covered box.

Merrill opened the box. A lapis lazuli choker nestled in the white satin folds. "I love lapis." The beads were cold against her fingers. They grew warm as she handled them.

"They match your eyes."

"They're beautiful." She held them to her throat. "Where did you get them?"

He took the beads from her and carefully slid them around her throat. "Eulalie gave me all her jewelry before she died."

He gently kissed the back of her neck, his lips hot.

"Please, don't kiss me like that." Merrill twisted around to face him. Every nerve ending tingled. She could still feel the imprint of his kiss on her neck.

He drew her into his arms. "After last night, I don't need a reason."

She twisted away from him. "I want you, Jason. But things are so complicated."

"Complicated, how? I'm a man. You're a woman. We want each other. What's simpler than that?"

"My grandmother—"

"Listen," Jason said, "you're all grown-up. It's time you started making your own decisions on how you want to live your life."

"Until this cotillion is over and Psyche is safe, I have to focus all my energy on them. Once everything is settled, you and I will sit down and hash out our relationship."

"What's to hash out? I love you. And, I think, you love me."

Officer Barnett, in plain clothes, stood in the doorway. "Excuse me, but everything is set up. It's time to drop off the money."

The undercover cops waited at the bottom of the stairs. They had decided against wiring her for sound because after she dropped off the money, she'd have to run to Blythe's and she wouldn't have time to worry about giving it all back. Instead, they'd wired Jason with a small microphone that could easily be removed once the operation was ended.

The police had provided Jason and Merrill with twenty duffel bags. Only two were filled with money–ten thousand dollars in one dollar bills, drawn on the dog's trust account. The remainder of the bags contained shredded newspaper. The bank, in a gesture to Eulalie's memory, had been very cooperative when Merrill had visited earlier in the day. The cop opened the front door, and Jason and Merrill stepped down the stairs to the driveway.

The duffel bags had been tossed into the back of Jason's truck. Jason opened the passenger door and helped Merrill into the truck, shoving the hem of her dress inside.

"Miss Prescott," one of the cops said, catching the door before Jason could close it, "remember, let him incriminate himself. If Mr. Bidwell is armed, you know what to do."

"I doubt he'd carry a gun. J.D. would shoot his foot off."

The cop smiled thinly. "We can't take chances. Just get the dog, and get out of there. We'll handle the rest."

Merrill smiled at him. "Thank you again for helping us."

"Our pleasure. We haven't had this much fun in a long time." He closed the door, grinning.

Jason started the truck.

The drive to the church was silent. Merrill didn't want the entire Charleston police force to know the state of her love life. The streets, packed with tourists staring at the historical houses and crossing the streets without looking, made navigation difficult. They were late.

The church was lit for the weekly choir rehearsal. Jason parked in the *no parking* zone, and Merrill opened the door and stepped out. Jason went to the back of the truck and pulled out one of the bags containing the money. He handed it to Merrill. The duffel was heavy.

As she pulled it up the steps, Merrill tried to pinpoint exactly when her life had taken this serious detour. Between falling in love and paying the ransom, she was way off course. She glanced at Jason. This was his fault. And all he could do was tell her to grow up and that he loved her. She felt like kicking him in the shins. Grow up, indeed. Of course, she loved him. Right now, she was a little busy. Men were so impatient. They wanted everything right here and now.

At the top of the steps, she saw Psyche's Folly tethered to a post. Next to the dog stood a man, dressed completely in black, a huge fake mustache under his nose and a black hat pulled down over a bad looking wig. She had always known J.D.'s elevator didn't go all the way to the top. Now, she suspected it didn't even get off the ground floor.

She dragged the duffel bag up the stairs while trying to hold her dress up to keep from tripping over the hem. At the sight of her, Psyche started barking and pulling at the leash.

"It's about time," J.D. growled in a voice as fake as his mustache.

Merrill was glad he hadn't succumbed to the temptation of fake glasses and a funny nose. She had to rein in her laughter. "Do you know how long it takes to find fifty million dollars in one dollar bills?"

"I said small bills, not one dollar bills."

"Beggars can't be choosers," she snapped.

Jason dropped his duffel bags and knelt to untie Psyche.

J.D. gestured at Jason. "What did you bring him here for?"

"Did you think I was going to carry all this money by myself through a city filled with strangers, in a ball gown? Look at me, J.D. Do I look dressed for intrigue? Either shut up and help us, or wait here while we drag the rest of the bags up, making a spectacle of ourselves. I feel like a misfit from a circus side show."

J.D. poked a hand in his pocket and a small bulge appeared. "Get the money, or I kill the dog."

Jason unclipped the leash. "In the truck, Psyche." He pointed, and the dog bounded down the steps and jumped into the bed of the truck. Jason faced J.D. "Forget the gun and killing the dog. Just help us. You know Merrill's grandmother better than I do. Do you want to be late for the party, too, J.D.?"

"I'm not J.D.," J.D. objected.

"Right," Merrill said. "Help us unload the damn bags."

"After I count the money."

"Are you crazy?" Merrill cried. "Do I look like I have the time to wait around for that?"

J.D. looked confused.

Jason shoved one of the duffel bags down the steps. "Listen, why not just take the whole damn truck?"

J.D. stared at the truck. "But isn't that stealing?"

Merrill started laughing and, once started, couldn't stop. "I don't think I'd worry." She lifted the hem of her skirt and kicked one of the bags. It tumbled, end over end, down the steps.

"Stop kicking my money."

"Quiet," Merrill commanded. "Or I'll do the same to you. I'm not in the mood for your antics."

They started down toward the truck, shoving the other three bags in front of them.

J.D. stood uncertainly on the curb, his hands in his pockets. He couldn't stand still, dancing around in a little circle like an Indian at a war dance. He pulled his hand out of his pocket, and Merrill saw the gleam of the gun in his hands.

Jason dug into his pocket and tossed the keys. Something gold gleamed with the keys. J.D. caught the keys and immediately dropped them to the pavement, screeching, "Ow!"

He held his hand out, and Merrill saw a red, round burn on his skin.

A gold coin rolled toward Merrill. She bent over and scooped it up. The coin tingled against her hand, but it didn't burn.

"Guess that's my lucky coin," Jason said.

Merrill handed it to him and he put it back in his pocket.

"You hurt me." J.D. sucked on the burn. "On purpose."

"J.D., get going," Jason ordered. "Psycho, down."

The dog jumped out of the truck and obediently sat at Jason's side.

J.D. jumped in the truck and gunned the motor. As J.D. squealed away from the curb, Merrill turned to Jason, "I guess we're going to have to hoof it. Wouldn't you know, I forgot my running shoes."

Jason held out his arm for Merrill to hold. They had started down the street when a white Lincoln Continental, a South Carolina State flag fluttering on the hood, stopped at the curb.

The window rolled smoothly down. "Miss Merrill?"

Merrill leaned into the window. "Chief Whitcomb. Mrs. Whitcomb."

The Chief of Police pushed the door open. "Hop in. Now that the operation is ended, we're on our way to your grandmother's cotillion. May we offer the three of you a ride?"

Jason opened the back door. "You don't mind taking the dog in you car?"

Mrs. Whitcomb smiled. "We'd be pleased to take the dog. If your grandmother won't mind."

"The dog has more money than a Third World country. I'm sure she'll make an exception," Merrill replied.

Everyone laughed.

Merrill's feet were saved, and she didn't have to speak to Jason. The scene in her bedroom had played over and over in her head until she thought she would go mad. He loved her, and she knew she loved him, but the war inside her would not end. Duty to family. Love for Jason. Back and forth, her emotions battled.

Eleven

During his marriage, Jason had seen plenty of formal gatherings in New York, but none compared to the Prescott Family Cotillion. It was the granddaddy of them all. The drive to the house was lined with Chinese lanterns waving gently in the evening ocean breeze. The gardens twinkled with white Christmas lights. Laughter and music bubbled out from the ballroom to the surrounding areas.

A valet opened the doors for Merrill and Mrs. Whitcomb. They stepped out onto the walkway to the portico. Jason watched as Merrill gracefully climbed the steps and then turned to look at him. Her lips curved up in the sweetest smile he'd ever seen, and she held out her gloved hand to him.

Jason clipped the dog's leash on and handed Psycho over to the valet. "Take care of her for me, will you? I'll get her back later."

He half stumbled up the steps. He wanted Merrill in his arms, in his life, in his bed. He couldn't get to her fast enough.

Inside, chairs lined the ballroom. Huge floral arrangements decorated the corners and sat on pedestals behind the buffet table. Five men in white tuxedos played instruments on a podium at one end of the room.

Blythe Prescott, with Carter Rutledge-Shelby, descended on Merrill and Jason.

Merrill's gaze roamed the room. "Nana, it's wonderful. Everything is so perfect."

"My investment is going to be returned tonight." She cast a satisfied glance at Carter.

Carter took Merrill's hand and tucked it around his forearm. "The next dance is reserved for us. Excuse us, Mr. Stavros, but I am borrowing Miss Prescott for a moment."

Carter drew Merrill onto the dance floor and whirled her effortlessly into a graceful waltz. Jason felt a surge of jealousy so great he almost choked.

"Aren't they beautiful together?" Blythe sighed, her hands clasped to her chest. "So perfect. I couldn't hope for a more wonderful son-in-law."

"Son-in-law!" Jason choked out. *No, Merrill, was his!*

"Grand-son-in-law, actually. Nothing is official yet, but after tonight ...." She winked at Jason.

"You're kidding, right?" He remembered the sable coat gift and Merrill's angry reaction to it.

Blythe rounded on him, her face set in firm lines. "Carter is Merrill's kind of people. My kind of people."

"Does Merrill know this?"

She frowned at him. "Merrill realizes that sometimes desire and duty are not the same thing. And when the two clash, duty will always win."

How archaic! Was this woman living in the seventeenth century? People didn't arrange marriages any more. "Do you love your granddaughter?"

"Of course, I do."

"Then how can you stand here and sell her to the highest bidder?"

She took a deep breath, her head high, her eyes flashing. "I do not have to explain myself to you, young man."

"Yes, you do. I'm in love with Merrill, and I'll be damned if I will let you sell her like a piece of property."

"She is property." Blythe's chin rose. "You think you are so sophisticated in your thinking. The world has never changed. Especially for people like us."

"What makes you so special?"

Her eyes flashed anger. "Our status. Our good name. Merrill is a beautiful woman from an old, aristocratic family. It doesn't matter we don't have money. To belong to the Prescott family of Charleston gives you privilege, prestige and power. Something you will never understand. I love my granddaughter, Mr. Stavros, and I will do what I must to ensure her future."

Jason couldn't believe he was hearing this. Did this old woman really believe what she said? Or was she just trying to justify her actions. "You mean *your* future."

"You're looking at me as though I've committed some heinous crime."

"I feel sorry for you, Mrs. Prescott. Merrill told me a little bit about her parents, and I know you forced her into a role you wanted your son to fill. He escaped, and Merrill, the loving compassionate person she is, will do anything to ensure your happiness at the expense of her own."

"You're wrong. Merrill will be happy. She'll have everything she wanted. She could even go back and work in the District Attorney's office if she wants to, although I can't understand why she'd want to."

"If Mr. Moneybags over there pays for her, he's going to demand she do exactly what he paid for. Everything that makes Merrill the wonderful person she is will be squashed. You'll have to live the rest of your life knowing you played a role in that."

She tossed her head, and opened her mouth to say something. But no words came out.

Jason didn't realize he'd been holding his breath. Where the hell did all that come from? He'd never been an introspective person, but his love for Merrill had given him courage. He'd faced off with Blythe Prescott and made her blink. Now all he had to do was stop Carter Rutledge-Shelby from forking over the big bucks.

A woman tapped on Blythe's shoulders. "Excuse me. Can you help me?" She was pregnant, and by the looks of her, almost ready to deliver. She wore a simple black dress. Golden hair was piled high on her head. He looked into her eyes and blinked in disbelief. For a second he thought he saw a thousand snakes, writhing in their depths.

"Pardon me, dear, but I don't recall your name," Blythe said in a polite but distant tone.

The pregnant woman's voice was loud and strident. "I'm Tess Rutledge-Shelby. I've come to find my husband, Carter. My baby needs his daddy." She burst into tears.

A second and third woman approached, one holding two children by the hands. "I'm Megan Rutledge-Shelby, and my babies need their daddy. I need my husband more."

Blythe grew pale and clutched at her chest. Jason grabbed her before she fell. The old woman's body shook like a rattle. He swore he could hear her bones knocking together.

A hush fell across the people nearest them. Jason saw their faces turned avidly toward the women.

"I'm Allie Rutledge-Shelby," the third woman said, waving her left hand with a huge diamond ring and matching band on it. "I don't have any babies, but Carter sure likes to be my sugar daddy." She strutted and waved at Carter. "Hey there, Sugar. I bought that cheerleading uniform you liked so much."

Blythe fainted dead away. Jason swung her up in his arms.

Merrill rushed across the dance floor. "What is going on?"

Jason tilted his head at the three women. "These women are all married to Carter."

Carter pushed through the growing crowd. "Don't be ridiculous. I don't know who these women are!"

A fourth woman pushed through. "Of course you do, Daddy. This is Tess. This is Megan. And this is Allie."

Jason shifted Blythe in his arms. "Who are you?"

The fourth woman snapped her fingers. "Some people call me the Goddess of Love." She shimmered with a silver radiance.

Carter pointed a finger at the fourth woman. "You're not supposed to be here."

The woman wriggled her fingers. "Gee, Daddy, I guess the hands-off policy didn't apply to you."

Jason was confused. "Time out. What the hell is going on here?" Blythe moaned as her head lolled back and forth.

"All of you shut-up," Merrill yelled. "I need a doctor for my grandmother. Mrs. Whitcomb, would you take these women into the parlor and get these poor children fed. Chief Whitcomb, you need to speak with this man." Merrill waved her hands at the crowd. "Everybody dance." Merrill snapped her fingers at the orchestra. "Play."

The musicians obediently started a tune, and she pushed Jason toward the French doors opening to the veranda. As he headed outside into the cooler night air, she grabbed two flutes of champagne.

"Marry me, I love you," Merrill said to Jason as he lowered her grandmother onto a wicker chaise. She set the flutes on a side table.

"What?"

"You heard me." She grabbed him by the lapels. "Marry me. I need you to protect me from all this craziness."

"Tell me you love me again." Jason stopped and repositioned the old lady.

"I love you, Jason Stavros."

He inclined his head toward Carter Rutledge-Shelby and the police chief heading toward the library. "And Carter?"

"I think he's already married—three times, apparently." She kissed him hard on the lips.

Blythe groaned and raised a hand to her forehead. "No."

Merrill smiled at Blythe. "Nana, it would be entirely inappropriate for me to marry a man who already has three wives and two and half children."

"But." Blythe pointed at Jason. "You don't understand."

Merrill fell to her knees in front of her grandmother. Jason hovered protectively over her, still not certain he'd heard Merrill right.

"Nana." Merrill took one of grandmother's lined hands in hers. "Nana, are you feeling better? Did you hit your head?"

"No," Blythe said, "let me speak. I want you to be happy. Jason is quite correct. I was wrong to insist you marry that man. Not only because he already is married, but because this young man here loves you with all his heart. He stood up to me like your father always has. I can respect that. I'll go to my grave denying I ever said this, but love is more important than money." Blythe struggled to her feet. She kissed Merrill on the cheek. "You be happy, Moon Beam."

"Moon Beam?" Jason asked as Blythe walked away.

Merrill blushed. "The baggage that children of hippies carry around with them."

Jason folded his arms around her and kissed her. He couldn't stop kissing her. Suddenly he wanted to be back at Eulalie's in that big old bed making love to this woman. "Let's go home."

She sighed. "Afraid not, Jason. We're going to have to stay. My grandmother spent a lot of money on this cotillion. I'm determined to enjoy it and eat as much food as I can. Besides, we'd better be here when she announces our engagement." She snuggled against him. "What did you say to make her change her mind?"

"I made her an offer she couldn't refuse."

"You've been watching too many Scorsese films."

"You bet." He kissed her again. Her lips were fire. She was a goddess in his arms, her body soft and ripe. He'd never make it to midnight. He wondered how many bedrooms Blythe had, and if any of them were empty.

Merrill touched his cheek. Her fingers were like flames against his skin. Jason didn't know what gods to thank for bringing Merrill into his life. But her love made him into more than he thought he could be.

He foresaw a long, happy marriage for them. And a love that would endure. Somewhere in the dark, he heard Psycho bark. She sounded as though she approved.

***

Venus sat perched on the edge of a chair. She could hardly sit still while her daddy tried to get himself out of his mortal fix. The Chief of Police hovered over him, screeching like a banshee. She loved it.

She snapped her fingers, and the Chief froze in position. Venus, Cupid, and Jupiter dissolved back into their natural state.

"I got rid of the Furies," Cupid said in his mother's ear.

"Thanks, Cupie." Venus wagged a finger in front of her father's face. "Daddy, we have to talk."

Jupiter drew himself up to his full height. "How dare you disobey me! Just because you're my daughter and I've given you the run of the heavens, doesn't mean that you can defy me."

Cupid resisted the urge to cower. When his grandfather went on a rampage, the only defense was cowardice.

Venus leaned forward, hands on her hips. "Well, excuu-uuse me." She glared at him. "You're the one who issued this silly hands-off policy, throwing the whole Pantheon into an uproar, just because you said mortals didn't need us anymore. Well, it turns out that 'Big Daddy, King of the Heavens' just wanted a little nookie and didn't want me interfering in his plans."

Jupiter held out his hand. "Now, kitten."

"Don't you kitten me, you libidinous old wind bag."

Cupid nudged his mother's elbow. "Ma, you're going too far."

"Quiet, Cupie," Venus snapped. "I have him where I want him."

He jostled her elbow again. "Ma. Don't push. You're winning this round."

Venus ignored him. She glowered at her father. "You made a promise to me when you interfered with Solomon and Sheba that you would let me do my job, my way. No fancy edicts. No more interference. And what do you do? You micro-manage me."

Cupid gaped at her. *Micro-manage! Where did she learn that term?*

"But, Baby," Jupiter cried, "you don't understand a man's needs."

"Oh, puh-lease." She took a deep breath. "I tried to understand about Sheba. I tried to understand about Eve. When you put on the silly serpent suit, do you realize you ruined it for everybody?"

Jupiter looked away. "You can't blame Sheba and Eve on me."

Venus stamped her foot. "Yes, I can."

Cupid could only admire his mother. But boy, this was getting ugly, bringing up stuff three thousand years in the past.

Jupiter took a stand. "I'm the boss here, young lady, and you will not speak to me in that tone of disrespect ever again."

Venus flicked her hand in his face. She was on roll and not about to stop. "Whatever."

"That's it," he thundered. The glass in the windows rattled. The frozen Chief Whitcomb shook where he stood. "I invoke the sacred rite of the Titans."

"Whatever you want, you low rent, petty dictator." Venus shrugged. "What can you do to me?"

Cupid shut his eyes. He could just feel himself on the way to becoming God of Slugs, Snails and Slime.

Lightning flashed around Jupiter's head. "You're demoted."

Venus tossed her head. "Been there, done that."

Rage flashed across Jupiter's face.

Cupid raised his chubby hand. "Sir? Grandpa?"

Jupiter eyed him sternly. "And you, too, fly boy."

"You can't demote me." Venus stood right up to him, feet apart. She even sprouted a few inches to stand nose to nose with her father.

"Yes, I can. Goddess of Fruit Trees and Garden Benches."

She backed up, aghast. "No."

"Oh yes." Jupiter smiled an evil smile. "Just call yourself the Fruit Tart."

Venus grew pale. Her mouth gaped open and closed.

Cupid's wings fluttered in agitation. He patted her cheek. "Ma, are you okay? Talk to me."

"And you," Jupiter pointed a finger at Cupid. "We're going to call you 'Goat Boy' from now on." A flash of thunder rolled through the room. Lightning sparked. A whirlwind appeared. The frozen mortal policeman toppled over with a thud.

Stark fear filled Cupid. He felt his wings shrivel. His legs lengthened, growing long and bony and covered with coarse hair. He stared down at the goat hooves that tapped a tattoo on the floor. "Baa!" he bleated, and slapped his hand over his mouth. Knobby horns pushed their way through the skin at the edge of his hairline. The pain was excruciating.

Jupiter clapped his hands. "Begone, both of you. I have had enough of this."

With a pop, Venus and Cupid floated upward, through the open window and into the sky.

Cupid glared at his mother. "I told you not to antagonize him, Ma."

Venus shrugged. "Okay. Okay. Maybe I did go a little overboard. Trust me." Venus smiled. "This is all temporary." She reached into her bodice and pulled out a piece of fruit. "Have a peach. We did our job, Cupie. We have nothing to apologize for, and I have a plan."

Cupid didn't want to know about her plan. He took the peach, bit into the rich meat and closed his eyes. The future looked bleak. He had nothing to look forward to. Another 'Baa' erupted from his lips. He was never going to live this down. The wood nymphs would be laughing at him for centuries. And to top it all off, he'd have to live outside in the woods. Cupid hated camping.

Epilogue

Jason and Merrill lay at the edge of the mattress, eating peaches and drinking champagne. Psyche, Buster and all the puppies sat in a row, tails wagging, eyes firmly fixed on Merrill and Jason.

"Do you think," Jason addressed the row of animals, "that I could spend my wedding night alone with my wife?"

Merrill giggled. The light from the lamp bounced off her wedding band. A simple gold band. She had no need for diamonds. Jason was all she ever needed. She snuggled against him.

Buster barked. He looked inordinately pleased with himself, and Merrill wondered why. Buster nuzzled Psyche, and the two lay down on their rug.

Merrill laughed. "I believe that's a no." Jason's body pressed tight against hers. She loved the feel of him.

"I had to try."

She tossed her peach pit into a bowl and sipped her champagne. Merrill had no idea she could be this happy, this contented. Her whole body tingled with the love she had for this man.

The door bell rang. Merrill frowned. "Who would interrupt us on our wedding night?"

Jason laughed. "Your grandmother. I told you we should have gone to Hawaii."

"Who's going to take care of the children?" She waved her hand at the line of puppies. They had all flopped into a heap and finally fallen asleep.

Jason patted her on the rump. He stood and grabbed his robe, tying the belt with a loose knot. "Don't move. I'll get rid of whoever it is."

Merrill took another sip of champagne. She stretched out on the bed waiting for Jason. Eyes closed she relived the day, the church filled to capacity with flowers and guests. Her grandmother reveling in the act of playing hostess. And even her parents had put aside their beads and sandals for formal wear and tradition.

Merrill smiled. She stretched her hand out and looked at her ring again. That simple band meant more to her than anything.

Jason returned, carrying a box. She sighed. "More puppies?"

"Not exactly."

He put the box on the bed. Merrill heard a sleepy meow. She reached in and pulled out one of the kittens. The black and white kitten nestled against the palm of her hand. She gently stroked it and then returned it to the box.

Merrill smiled at Jason. "What are we going to do with cats?"

"We'll think of something." He kissed her, deep and probing. "Right now, I have plans for you, Mrs. Stavros."

She scooted a little closer until their naked bodies touched. Whatever plans he had were okay with her.

A Special Preview
of
J. M. Jeffries

Cupid:
The Captivating Chauffeur

Coming in
September, 2000

Prologue

Venus sneezed. She sat on her couch trying not to cry. She hadn't known she had allergies. All this pollen was making her puffy. Eight mortal months since she'd been demoted. She hated being the Goddess of Fruit Trees and Gardens. Her eyes were swollen, her skin blotchy, and her nose was runny. Cupid was no help. All he did was scratch since he'd been made God of the Flocks and Shepherds. He talked about nothing but his fleas and ticks. She sneezed again.

Cupid appeared in a cloud of smoke. "Mom, are you all right?"

"Do I look all right? The next time you maneuver me into defying my father, I'll... I'll... I don't know what I'll do, but I'll do something."

"Excuse me. Goddess of Love. Mother of Cupid. You're the one who said Jupiter's 'hands off humans' policy was a disaster waiting to happen."

"If I hadn't already decided on a soul mate for Merrill Prescott, I probably would have never interfered. My father had no right meddling in my affairs of the heart. I'm the Goddess of Love and Romance."

"It's all about your ego, isn't it Mom? Look at me. I'm a goat."

"Look at you!" Venus sobbed. "Look at me. I'm wearing green leaves. I hate green. I hate flowers. I hate fruits. I'm expected to play in the dirt. Do you know how hard it is to get dirt out from under my fingernails?" She splayed her hands, showing broken fingernails. "My manicurist won't even take me anymore."

"Like your life is so bad." He held up one horned hoof. "Look at that. I have cloven hooves for feet." He ran a hand over his head. "I have horns." He touched his hips. "I have fur jockey shorts. I haven't had a date in months."

Venus jumped to her feet. "You haven't had a date! Daddy expects me to grow dates, not get them." She snapped her fingers and a piece of fruit appeared in her hands. "Look at this! I don't even know what it is."

"It's a pomegranate."

"Do I look like Farmer Jane?" She glared at the offending piece of fruit. "Do you think I know what I'm doing?"

"That's pretty obvious. The tabloids are still trying to explain cucumbers growing from the branches of the apple trees in Washington."

She wiped her tears away. "I didn't know apples were supposed to grow from those branches. I watched Martha Stewart, not the farm report. All I know is how to make a planter from a truck tire."

Cupid patted her knee. "Don't worry, Mom. This can't possibly last forever. Grandpa hasn't gotten a replacement for you yet."

She perked up. "Who could replace me?" A surge of hope sprang up inside her.

"No one, Mom."

"I'm the only one, besides you, who truly knows about love. It's who I am, what I do. How are you doing, darling?"

"Still trying to explain those sheep on Antarctica." He shrugged. "They were wearing coats. I thought they'd be fine. Who knew they'd end up as sheep-cicles?"

A bell rang. Venus crossed her arms. "You answer the door. If it's Daddy, I don't want to speak to him. *EVER*." She turned her back and glared at the wall.

She heard Cupid's hooves click across the marble floor and the door open.

"Mom," he called, "it's Great Aunt Vesta."

Venus turned to face her aunt. Vesta was a tall woman, rail thin and almost gaunt looking. She looked like the road from Athens to Rome – not a curve on her. The knot of hair on top of her head was so tight, her eyes looked stretched, as though she'd had twenty face lifts in the last six months. Her lips were pinched and narrow.

Vesta, the paragon of virtue and morality, wore a pristine white turtleneck toga which covered every inch of her body. Not one bit of skin other than face and hands showed.

"Aunt Vesta, come to gloat." Venus tried not to sound bitter.

"No, dear," Vesta said in her whiny little voice. "I need some advice."

Venus almost fainted. "Are you trying to catch a man?"

Vesta looked astonished. "I never ...."

Venus waved a hand. "Maybe you should."

Cupid burst out laughing.

Vesta stamped her foot. "I did not come here to be the butt of your licentious humor."

"Baaa! I'm sorry, Great Aunt Vesta," Cupid said with a mortified squeak.

"So what's on your mind?" Venus demanded.

Vesta tapped her fingers on her arm. "Your father, in all his mighty wisdom, has made me you."

"I beg your pardon."

"Jupiter finally decided on who was to replace you. I am now the Goddess of Love." For a second, she looked transported. "I can hardly believe it. I'm being given a chance to show what I can do." She clasped her hands to her heart.

"You're the Goddess of Love." Venus felt a spurt of fury. "Daddy replaced me with you. You—the queen of pristine, the princess of purity, the viscountess of virginity."

"Yes. This is my chance to remake the world into my own chaste image."

Venus could only stare. "Oh, my gods. Oh, myself." She had to sit down. Not that she could find a comfortable spot with all these leaves on her derriere. "Cupie. Fetch me a glass of water. I think I'm going to wilt."

"I will not allow you to faint," Vesta cried. "I need your assistance."

Cupid snapped his fingers, and a glass of water appeared. He threw the water on Venus. Her leaf dress perked up a bit. Vesta looked mildly perturbed. Or maybe that was a smile. Venus was never sure. "Why should I help you?" Venus crossed her arms. "You have my job."

"It's no fault of mine you were reassigned. If you'd obeyed my brother, you wouldn't be paying the consequences now."

Venus held up her hand. "Excuse me, you make him sound like some pious old windbag. He isn't. I forgot, your job is to make him into something more holy than he is. But if you're now me, that isn't your job any more."

Vesta preened. "I will be doing double duty as both Goddess of Love and Goddess of Virtue and the Hearth."

Venus stared at her aunt. "You get two prime jobs, and I have to grow apricots on vines?"

Cupid touched her arm. "Apricots grow on trees, Mom."

"Whatever." She rubbed her forehead. "I can't stand this pressure."

Vesta looked annoyed. "I have no time for your emotional outbursts, Venus. I thought you and I could finally bury the hatchet."

"Right in your head," Venus muttered.

"Ma!" Cupid said in warning.

She shrugged. "What?"

"Be nice."

Vesta whirled around. "You know what? I don't need your help. I can do this. I can make people fall in love better than you, and still maintain some modicum of decorum and morality. No more running off to the woods to do who knows what. I never did like the way you let people gallivant about doing whatever they wanted." She shuddered.

"Say it," Venus spat out.

"Say what?" Vesta looked confused.

"You know. The nasty. The old bump and grind. The naked fandango." She snapped her finger. "The wild thing."

Vesta clutched her throat, her fingers pale against the knitted edge of her turtleneck toga. She gasped, "I don't have the faintest idea what you mean."

Venus shook her finger at her aunt. "That's the problem. You cannot make people fall in love without understanding bodily desires."

Choking, Vesta clutched at her arms. "Sex!"

"Welcome to the real world." Cupid jumped up and down. "Give the prude a prize."

Vesta shook herself. "I am going to remake the world. When women were virgins and men were honorable."

"This I've got to see." Venus muttered to her son.

"I've had enough of your insolence, Venus. I've already decided on my first love match—Olivia Montgomery and Andrew Sullivan."

"Andrew needs someone much more fun-loving than that."

Vesta raised an eyebrow. "That is no longer your concern."

Watch me get concerned. Venus grinned at her aunt. "Don't let the door hit your backside on the way out."

"Sticks and stones may break my bones, but nothing penetrates my chastity belt." Vesta knocked on her hip, and the sound of metal clanged throughout the room.

Cupid rolled his eyes. Venus pointed at the door. "Begone, you dried up old nag."

Cupid snickered, and the snicker became a long drawn out baa. When they were alone, Venus hugged herself. "Well, we won that one didn't we, Cupie."

Cupid only shrugged. "Maybe. She still has your job."

"Not for long. You and I are going on a mission."

"Mom, we're demoted. And the Tribunal has not revoked my promotion just because I'm demoted." He looked at his cloven hooves again.

Venus thought he needed a pedicure and a trip to Vulcan's Smithy. She jumped to her feet and paced back and forth. "Fine. Fine. I'll be their garden goddess, fruit-picking Susie Cream Cheese, but I'm not going to stop making love matches just because I'm now the official 'hoe' queen." She held out a hand, and a fish bowl with strips of yellow paper in it appeared in her palm. Emblazoned across the side of the bowl in gold gilt were the words, *New York City—female.*

Cupid frowned. "Mom, I can hear the hamster spinning its wheel in your head."

"What hamster?" She touched her hair.

"Never mind, Ma. You have a plan." His shoulders slumped. "You're going to find a match for Andrew, aren't you? Go ahead. I'm in. I'll save myself the aggravation and give in now."

Venus smiled at him. "Thank you, Son." She reached into the bowl and picked out a name. She read from the paper strip. "Francesca Ling. I like that name."

She glared at the heavens. Clenched in her fist, she held the name high above her head. "I'm going to prove, once and for all, that there is only one Goddess of Love and her name is Venus. We shall regain our rightful place."

Cupid frowned. "How much further down in the food chain can we go? God of Leeches and Swamp Fungus?"

She kissed him on the cheek. "You worry too much. Come on. Let's go." Venus disappeared in a flash of lightning and thunder heading toward New York City.

One

Andrew Sullivan walked briskly, sunlight fading as the sun dipped down toward the horizon. His life felt empty. After fifteen years of raising his brothers and sister and making his millions, he had no more goals. His youngest sibling, Patrick, had just graduated *magna cum laude* from Columbia and gone off to make a life for himself.

What was Andrew supposed to do with his life now? He didn't need money. He had more then enough for ten lifetimes. He didn't need to be a father anymore. His brothers and sisters were all grown up, some with families of their own, and others starting on their life paths. He had nothing left to do.

He unknotted his tie. Yesterday, he'd sold his brokerage firm. He would never again have to wear a suit. Maybe he should marry, like his sister Colleen urged, and have lots of little Sullivan babies.

My God, what am I thinking? He'd just gotten rid of the last one. He didn't want another family to raise. He wanted to have fun. When was the last time he'd had fun? Either he had a stock proposal to put together, a PTA meeting to attend, groceries to buy, or school counselors to talk with. He wanted to kick up his heels. Here he was, thirty-seven years old, wanting to feel like he was back in high school with a cool car, a hot chick, and nothing more on his mind but avoiding cops, getting drunk and getting laid.

Maybe he should go back to school and finish his degree. Right. He could see himself sitting in a classroom with a bunch of eighteen-year-olds, trying to understand the economic necessity for the Battle of Hastings. No way!

He turned down a side street. Kids in leather sets leaned against light poles with cigarettes dangling out the sides of their mouths. That could have been his future—aimless and wandering—if he hadn't been saddled with his brothers and sisters to care for after their parents' sudden death. But still, he felt a moment of longing for the carefree adventure of youth. He felt like an old man. Thirty-seven and half-way to the grave. He had nothing left to accomplish.

Lights twinkled in a vest-pocket park situated between two towering apartment buildings. Drew turned and looked for a place to sit. He needed time to think. He needed time to plan his future. When was the last time he'd sat in a park by himself without a brood of siblings to watch?

Sobbing broke the silence. He turned around, trying to see who was crying. The park was small and intimate, with fruit trees and a fountain at the center. Near the fountain an older woman sat, her hair covering her face, her hands over her eyes. She sobbed piteously.

Drew sat next to her. "Are you okay, ma'am?"

"I lost my job!" the woman cried.

She was neatly dressed in hideous green clothes that looked like jungle foliage. Though her clothes looked worn, they were neat and cared for. A mangy dog sat at her feet scratching its ear and shaking its head.

"Would you like to talk about it?" Andrew asked soothingly.

"My own father fired me." She raised her face. "And after all I've done for him."

Beneath the blotchy, puffy skin, he could see she was an attractive woman. Well-cared for. Not the type he expected to find sobbing in a park. "Tough break."

"Tell me about it." She rubbed her nose and honked into a Kleenex. "What am I supposed to do now?" She absently patted the dog's head. "And Cupid needs a flea dip." The dog shuddered and bounced away, scooting his rear end on the grass. "Everything was fine one day. The next day we have this tiny little disagreement, and I'm supposed to know how asparagus grows. Now tell me, how am I supposed to know that?"

Drew was lost. He had no clue where this conversation was going. He patted her on the shoulder. At least he could be sympathetic. "What kind of work do you do?"

"I'm sort of a couples coordinator." She wiped her eyes.

What the hell was that? "That sounds interesting. Exactly what is that?"

"You don't know?"

"I'm a retired stock broker. I haven't had time for much coordinating lately."

She shook her head. "That's too bad. You're a very handsome man. I've always liked men with red hair." She rolled her shoulders seductively, and little sparkles haloed her head. "I'm surprised some smart woman hasn't lassoed you and tied you down." She gave him a suggestive wink.

Drew was suddenly uncomfortable. He'd gone from sympathetic ear to perspective boy toy in only a second. He had no idea how the woman had twisted their positions so easily. The dog ran up and jumped in her lap. She pushed the animal away. "Get down, Cupid. I'm working here."

Drew stared at her. Maybe she was unstable. He needed to get away. "Listen," he handed her his business card. "Call this number. My friend will find you suitable employment." He dug out his wallet and gave her all his cash. "This money will tide you over until you're working again."

She looked astonished. She dug into her purse and handed him a small round object. "Keep it. It's for luck."

When he touched the object, an electrical shock coursed up his fingers, up his arm. His hair stood on end. "You don't need to give me anything."

The woman smiled. "Yes, I do. It's part of the bargain."

Before he could respond, she stood up and walked away, the little dog trailing in her wake. He glanced at the coin. Golden lights seemed to spark from it. When he looked up, the woman and dog had disappeared. Where had they gone? He whirled around, looking for them, but they were nowhere in sight.

He pocketed the coin. *What a strange way to end a very strange day.*

He walked back out onto the street. New York was truly the city that never slept. Traffic roared past him. Cabbies yelled at each other. A mounted police officer ambled along on the other side of the street. He watched the officer and his horse. A reflection off a window attracted him. *White Lotus Limousine Service.* A neon light flashed, *OPEN.*

Drew didn't know where the idea started, but before he'd even thought it through, he was opening the door and walking inside.

* * *

Francesca Ling bent over an open book. Next to her elbow, a dispatch radio blinked. She answered absently. Her uncle, Charles Ling, gave her his location and signed off. She logged it into the book. Five seconds later, her cousin Guido called in his location and she answered. Before she had a chance to finish his log, the door opened and a tall, red-headed man walked through it. Frankie stared at him and when he smiled at her, she practically fell off her chair. If he had asked her name, she wouldn't be able to tell him. Fortunately, she was wearing a name tag.

"Hello," he said. He squinted at her name tag. "Frankie, is it?"

"Hi," her voice trailed away into a breathy sigh. This man was every woman's fantasy. She wanted to run her hands through his wavy hair and kiss his sensual lips. Then reality returned. She stood up. "May I help you." Business first, her father was always telling her.

"Do you rent limousines for an extended period of time?"

"Uh, how long are you going to be in the city, sir?" She pushed black hair out of her face.

"Not for the city."

"Connecticut, then. No problem."

He shook his head. "I had something else in mind."

"I don't know New Jersey!" She hated driving to New Jersey. The drivers over there had no clue what the rules and regulations of the road entailed.

"I don't want to go to New Jersey."

He was cute, but he certainly didn't know from much. "Where then?"

"I'm thinking of something longer. Cross-country, maybe."

"Los Angeles! San Francisco!" Wow, what a cab fare that could earn. Her father would be rubbing his hands together. "So why not just rent a car from Hertz?"

He looked abashed, as though he'd been caught doing something naughty. "I don't drive."

Frankie stared at him. "You don't drive." She might not be able to find her way across the block, but she could drive. Her father told her she was directionally impaired, which was why she was on the radio at night. After dark, she could hardly find the damn car.

"Never had time to learn." He seemed to shake himself. "Excuse me, let me introduce myself. I'm Andrew Sullivan."

He's Andrew Sullivan! Her thoughts tumbled in a tangent. This was the fourth richest man in Manhattan. "You mean like *the* Andrew Sullivan as in Sullivan Brokerage?"

"Actually, that is formerly of Sullivan Brokerage, though the new investors are keeping the name. I'm retired now."

Frankie's eyes narrowed. "Retired. Why?" She had barely started her career in costume design, and he's retiring already. What a world! Her grandmother would have an old Chinese proverb to say, but at the moment, Frankie couldn't think of any of them. Actually, Frankie could think of them, but they always came out mutilated.

He shrugged. "I did what I wanted to do. Now I'm looking to play."

"You think driving across country is playing." Boy, she should be so lucky.

He opened his wallet and drew out a Platinum American Express. "I can pay."

"I know that." She eyed the credit card dubiously. She'd never seen one up close and personal before. She wanted to touch it, hoping some of his business sense would rub off on her. She barely qualified for a Discover Card, and her credit limit was only a thousand dollars. Here he was offering her the universe.

"I need to talk to the boss about this. Can I fix you some green tea?" According to her grandparents, green tea fixed everything.

"No thanks. But I appreciate the offer."

"Could you just wait a moment?" She waved at a plastic chair. Suddenly, she was too aware of the shabby look of the office, the fingerprints that were clearly visible on the glass door, and her own unorthodox appearance. Her long black hair hung straight down her back. She wore a leopard print mini-skirt, a black painter's smock, leopard beret, and patent leather Mary Janes–the ones she'd worn in high school at St. Joan's.

Frankie ran into her father's office. "Daddy." She closed the door and leaned back against it.

Her father liked to pretend he was old world Chinese, even though his great-great grandparents had come to the United States to work the railroad a hundred and twenty years ago, and the family had easily assimilated itself into American culture. He looked up, his eyes quizzical. "What's going on?"

"Dad, we have a live one."

"A live one, what?"

"Andrew 'I make Donald Trump look like a pauper' Sullivan is outside and wants to rent a limo and driver for a cross-country trek." She could almost see her dad mentally rubbing his hands together. If there was one thing her father liked, it was money.

"For how long?" he asked.

"How long does it take to drive to Los Angeles? Four, five days."

"Why not fly?"

Frankie threw her hair back. "I don't know. Like I'm going to ask him. I'm sure he has a good reason for what he wants to do."

Her dad stood, straightened his tie and pushed his hair back. "Bring him in, then."

Frankie opened the door and peeked out. Andrew Sullivan stood in the middle of the foyer staring out the window at the street.

"Mr. Sullivan," she said and opened the door wide, gesturing him in.

Andrew Sullivan filled the small office with his presence. Frankie shrank back into a corner trying to be inconspicuous. She watched as the two men shook hands. Andrew sat down. Her father stared at her, and with a jolt, she realized he wanted her to leave. Reluctantly, she left and went out to sit at the desk.

A cross-country trek, she thought. What a great adventure! She cupped her chin in her hand and gazed out the window. Boy, that sounded so exciting. Just pick and go. No responsibilities. No one to depend on you. No grandmother nagging you to tidy your bedroom. No mom to bring home every eligible bachelor between Little Italy and Chinatown. On the road, doing what she wanted, eating junk food.

The whole idea sounded like heaven. And to travel with someone like Andrew Sullivan! She bet he could show a girl a great time. His business exploits were legendary. His personal ones were just as hot. He was so beautiful, and he exuded such confidence.

She couldn't get her mind off him. Not that a man like him would ever look at a girl like her. She was Downtown, and he was Uptown. She was Chinese and Italian, small and dark. Every woman she'd ever seen him with on the pages of the society column was tall and blonde with a perfect body and perfect teeth. The only part of Frankie that was perfect were her teeth, and her parents had mortgaged both China and Italy to give them to her.

The door to her father's office opened. They shook hands, and Andrew tossed her a beautiful smile. Frankie's insides melted.

When he was gone, the office seemed dull and lifeless. Sort of like her personal life. "Dad, what happened?"

Her father turned. "He rented the Range Rover for four weeks."

"And who's going to drive him?"

"Uncle Marco."

"Daddy, you can't send Uncle Marco away for four weeks. His parole officer will never allow it." Besides which, Uncle Marco wasn't that great a driver.

Her father shrugged. "You let me work on that."

"You could have assigned me."

Her father started laughing. "First of all, Frankie, what happens if he wants to drive at night? You'll end up in Nova Scotia. Remember when I sent you to Long Island and you ended up in Pennsylvania?"

"The map was upside down."

"Yes, but a good driver would have noticed that." He disappeared back into his office, the door shutting on any other objections she might think of.

Frankie sat down. She would love to be stuck in a Range Rover with Andrew Sullivan for four weeks. But her father did have a point. She had a way of getting terminally lost. So much for the grand adventure. But she could dream.

##

Cupid turned around and took one more look at Andrew Sullivan. He couldn't blame his mom; Drew was a good-looking man. And Venus was Venus. Jupiter could make her the Goddess of Lint Balls, but she'd go on making matching and falling into lust.

His body shifted. Maybe this time, he'd shift back into his familiar cherub form. He could hope, but one look at his feet told him his hope was in vain. Cloven hooves appeared, and he was back to being a half goat. He hated being a goat. He hated forests. He hated dirt. He hated goats. Somehow, some way, he would get back in good with his grandfather.

"Francesca Ling," Venus said, "is going to have the adventure of a lifetime."

"Far be it from me to be critical, Ma, but aren't we out of the Love Game?"

She waved her hand in the air as the door to her palatial home swung open. "I'm the only one besides you, dear, who can do it right."

They stepped into the foyer. Boxes dotted the entry.

"Cupie," Venus frowned. "Am I redecorating?"

All the niches were empty. All the statues of his mother were gone. "Not that I know of, Ma." He glanced curiously upward. Even the crystal chandelier was gone. Something was definitely wrong here.

They walked into the main living area. Vesta stood in the center of the room, waving her hands at a chorus of Lares. The household gods and goddesses popped into the air and started hanging some dark, dreary picture of Vesta.

"Get that thing off my wall," Venus yelled.

Vesta whirled around. "This is my house now."

"No, it's not. I've lived here since the dawn of time, and I'll live here until the universe ends."

Vesta drew herself up, straight and tall. "Not anymore. This is house is part of my benefits package. I made sure Jupiter included it in my contract."

Cupid was stunned. "You have a contract?"

Vesta grinned. "Of course, you silly boy. Or is silly goat?" Her crackling laugh filled the room.

Venus turned around. "Where are my things?"

Vesta waved a hand at the entry. "Somewhere out there. I thought I'd have a garage sale. But then again, who would want all your trashy things with all the bordellos in Nevada closing down. Lack of business, I understand."

"You mean, you hope, you dried up old prune."

"Who is calling whom a prune?" Vesta's colorless eyes were filled with contempt.

Venus stamped her foot. "This is my house. Get out."

She crossed her arms over her chest. "I don't think so."

Cupid grabbed at his mother. "Ma, we'll worry about the house later. We have the 'thing' to take care of."

"What thing?"

"You know." Cupid tilted his head at the door. He whispered in her ear. "Francesca."

Venus looked confused for a moment, then she smiled. "Oh, I get it. The 'thing.'"

"Come on, Ma. We'll go crash with Minerva." He pulled Venus out of the room.

ABOUT THE AUTHOR

J. M. Jeffries is the pen name for writing team Jacqueline S. Hamilton and Miriam Pace.

Jacqueline is the proud owner of twenty-seven shades of red lipstick. At the ripe old age of twenty-three, she ran away from home to Europe and the Carribean to visit friends and relatives only because Ringling Brothers, Barnum and Bailey Circus wasn't accepting applications. She is living proof that at age eighteen one doesn't need to know what they want out of life. She is also living proof that at thirty five one doesn't need to know what they want out of life.

While she considers herself a happy person, Jackie fights daily with her envy issues. At college, she studied sociology because it was the only subject besides romance novels that attempted to explain the meaning of life. She considers herself a workaholic/procrastinator and would rather lay on the sofa patting her tummy, teaching her friend's dog how to smoke, and then lie about it. She is passionately enamored of Steven Spielberg's *Animaniacs*, William Faulkner novels, and "The New Detectives: a Study of Forensic Science" on the Discovery Channel.

Jackie decided to write romance novels because she can't sing, can't dance, it doesn't involve high math, nor must she wear high heels. She also believes that the body God intended to give her was misplaced on Jennifer Lopez. She believes in extra-terrestrial life, but doesn't want aliens visiting her at home. Jackie doesn't exercise because she believes the eleventh commandant is "Thou shall not sweat." You may e-mail Jackie at: hmltnjs@aol.com

**

Miriam is the only woman in the world with her own hand cream collection which she uses everywhere on her body except her hands. Her greatest beauty secret is lip balm for the elbows. She has the refinement of a Victorian lady, the intelligence of a Nobel Prize Laureate, and when the stars are straight and the moon is full, she has the vocabulary of a truck driver. Miriam truly believes the only reason she received a Masters Degree in English was because her instructors were too afraid she'd come back. She has been known to level mountain ranges with the lift of an eyebrow. But her friends consider her generous, warm and a closet dominatrix.

Miriam knew she would marry her husband of twenty-nine years after their first date, but made him wait a whole year before she said, "I do," so he could have the illusion he was the pursuer. She is known as the curator of the Pace Zoo. At any time one can find sheep in her back yard, a German Shepard mixbreed dog who thinks she's a cat, kamikaze koi with an attitude, a Russian Blue cat who redefines the word lazy, and a Persian who needs Prozac.

She knew she was destined to be a writer when she started receiving her first rejections in high school, and decided something was wrong with the editors. Acknowledged as the Goddess of All Things, Miriam is the first one everyone turns to when they need advice. You may e-mail Miriam at: Miriam@pe.net

Other Books Available from ImaJinn Books

A Love Through All Time by Jean Nash. $9.95

Swept into a spontaneous life regression, Andrea Morrow learns that her tragic past is being repeated. Can Andrea reverse the tide so that she and her soul mate can fulfill their destiny and share...A Love Through All Time?

Cupid: The Amorous Arrow by J. M. Jeffries $7.50

Cupid's in trouble with the Tribunal of the Gods. His punishment is to unite Amberlin O'Rourke and her kleptomaniac aunt with the loves of their lives. If he doesn't succeed Cupid could end up demoted to God of Dog Duty!

Dreamsinger by J. A. Ferguson $8.50

First Daughter Nerienne, heir to the Tiria of Gayome, faces the destruction of her world when her mother's enemies kill the Tiria. Nerienne is left with just her magic and with Bidge, a strange, shelled creature that speaks only to Nerienne. She is rescued by Durgan Ketassian, leader of the rebels in the northern woods, but can she trust this man whom her mother condemned to die?

Mad About Max by Holly Fuhrmann $8.50

Author, Grace Macguire, has a small problem with three of her characters, a trio of fairy godmothers. They've come to life! Myrtle, Fern and Blossom promise to make all of Grace's wishes come true, to include finding her her own Prince Charming. But all Grace wishes is that they will go away. Unfortunately, the bumbling fairies are here to stay.

Midnight Enchantment by Nancy Gideon $8.50

After a 400 year existence as a vampire, Gerard Pasquale wants only to be left alone to shadow the midnight streets of turn of the century New Orleans . . . until blackmail binds him to a mortal bride who throws his dark world into an upheaval.

Time of the Wolf by Julie D'Arcy $9.95

Brekan, Druid of the ancient order of Palandor sends Keahla, outlawed princess of Carrum Bahl, through a time portal to seek Radin Hawk, reincarnated soul of Ambroch, King of the Wolfhead. Brekan must join together the Selected Four on the night that the moons are as one to re-enact the ritual that can raise the Blood King, Czetan, from the undead. What begins as a quest to stop a Witch Queen from raising her lover to destroy a nation, becomes a battle against the dark side of human nature ... and a race against the crumbling gates of time.

ORDER FORM ON NEXT PAGE

ORDER FORM

Name:_____

Address:_____

City:_____

State_____ **Zip**_____ **Phone***_____

Qty	Book	Cost	Amount

Total Paid by:	SUBTOTAL	
☐ Check or money order	SHIPPING	
☐ Credit Card (Circle one) Visa Mastercard Discover American Express	MI Residents add 6% sales tax	
_____ Card Number	TOTAL	

_____
Expiration Date

_____
Name on Card

Would you like your book(s) autographed? If so, please provide the name the author should use_____

*Phone number is required if you pay by Credit Card

Shipping costs:
1 book $2.00
2-3 books $2.50
4-5 books $3.50
(Shipping prices for U.S. residents only. Foreign customers will be notified if we can ship to your country, and we'll get your approval of shipping charges prior to filling your order)

MAIL TO: ImaJinn Books, PO Box 162, Hickory Corners, MI 49060-0162

Or order on our web site at: http://www.imajinnbooks.com

Questions? Call us toll free: 1-877-625-3592